Billionaire Daddy's New Nanny
Billionaire Age Gap Sweet Romance

Kit O'Neal

CRB Publishing

Copyright © 2023 by Kit O'Neal

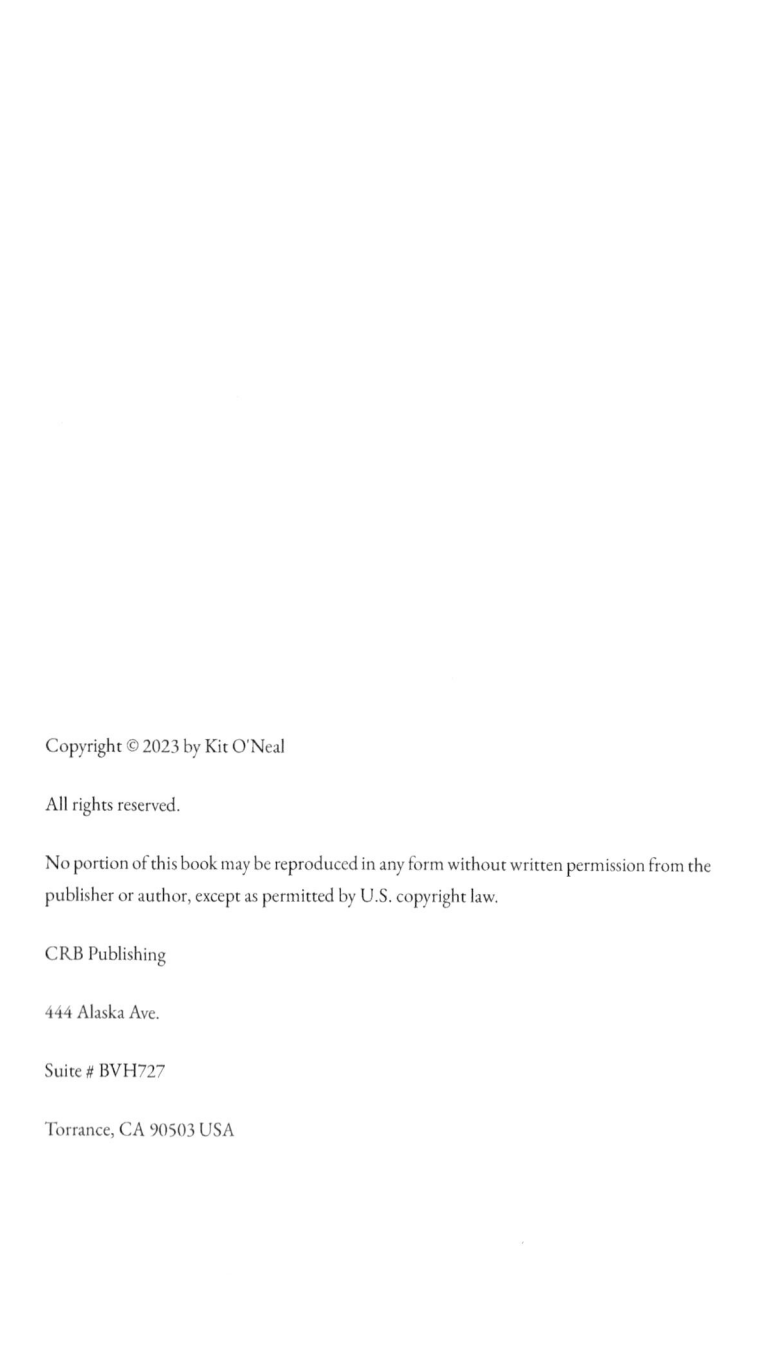

All rights reserved.

No portion of this book may be reproduced in any form without written permission from the publisher or author, except as permitted by U.S. copyright law.

CRB Publishing

444 Alaska Ave.

Suite # BVH727

Torrance, CA 90503 USA

Contents

1. Scott — 1
2. Daisy — 12
3. Scott — 24
4. Daisy — 34
5. Scott — 48
6. Daisy — 58
7. Scott — 67
8. Daisy — 77
9. Scott — 84
10. Daisy — 91

Chapter 1
Scott

"My son did *what*?" I nearly fell over my desk as I jumped from my chair. I had my phone pressed to my ear as if my life depended on it. "I'm sorry, say that again?"

"Mr. Wilson, we're holding your son here in the front office," said the tart voice on the other end of the phone. "Like I said before, well he—he uppercut one of his classmates. A verbal disagreement escalated and both boys were pulled into separate corners. The other boy has a busted nose, Mr. Wilson. Very serious."

"Uppercut?" I almost wanted to laugh, but I was worried it might sound like an unhinged person and that was the last thing I needed them to think. "I'll be at the school soon."

I had my driver take me, and my sleek, black town car slid through the streets. The paint glimmered off of buildings when the car passed by. The school was right in the middle of the city, and it was the kind of place that was way too prim and well-maintained to allow fighting on the play area or anywhere else in the school for that matter. To my horror, my twelve-year-old son had somehow become a city brawler in his off hours without me knowing. I almost couldn't believe it. Actually no, I definitely couldn't believe it with the way he had been acting out lately. I mean Cameron obviously had a tough six months, but he had never been violent toward anyone, not ever in his life. I had been to the school so many times in the past few months and knew the halls much better than I ever wanted to though. My son had never *hit* another person though. I couldn't help but sigh. He used to be such a mild kid.

"Mr. Wilson? Is that you?"

I recognized the bright, overly excited voice right away and I knew the young lady in the front office was about to check me out from head to toe. I felt bad, but I wasn't even sure of her actual name. I looked up, shooting her a polite smile. She twirled her limp, dark hair around her thin ring finger. She slid closer in her chair to the edge of the desk. She peeked over the computer, looking me up and down like she always did. It was awkward and obvious.

"Hi," I nodded, clearing my throat. "I'm here to meet with the principal about Cameron?"

"Such a sweet little guy!" She answered me way too quickly, nodding vigorously. "The counselor wanted to see him. I'm sure he's getting some kind of award. Best kid in middle school," she tittered.

I rubbed my fingers over my face. "Nope, he hurt another kid. He punched someone."

She seemed to go pale, turning right back to her computer. "Um, you can go back there, sir."

She obviously had no idea. You would think a nice, privately funded school would make an effort to tell all of their staff about the bar brawls going on outside by the slides and swings, but obviously not. I moved down the short hallway, taking in the tangy scent of some kind of citrus-smelling carpet cleaner. It smelled like a dentist's office to me. It was the first door on the left and before I raised my hand to knock, the door opened to let someone else come out.

"Oh, Mr. Wilson, thank goodness you're here I was just going to give you another call," a voice that I recognized as the principal called out, standing in the open door in her tan, fitted pantsuit. "Usually, parents aren't late when it comes to matters like this, but I suppose this will have to do."

She was a rigid, stone-faced woman and I assumed she had been military before beginning an eventual career with children. What an odd choice for a woman like that to make.

"I was only four minutes late," I told her, trying not to sound like a grumpy child. "There was traffic."

There was no traffic at all.

"Of course," she said, raising an eyebrow and apparently seeing right through me. "Please come on in and have a seat."

The man who was sitting at the desk was a wan, sallow-faced gentleman that I recognized as the school's guidance counselor. He was not a man I would want to get guidance from, but there we were, seeking his counsel.

"Hey, Dad," a bright voice said, and I saw Cameron sitting happily in one of the chairs in front of the desk, sucking on a peppermint from the half-full bowl. "Are you taking me home?"

"You and me, we'll talk later," I said, shushing him as I hustled to sit down in the uncomfortable chair next to him.

"Mr. Wilson, thank you for coming in today," Arthur Roland said, pushing his glasses up higher on his nose. "I'm afraid we need to discuss Cameron's behavior."

"Yes, I'm aware," I said, staring at him until he squirmed. "I left a very important meeting for this."

"With all due respect, your son being suspended from school and all related activities is just as important, if not more," said the woman behind me.

I could feel her staring at me, but I kept my eyes on the awkward man sitting at the desk.

"Suspended?" I asked, tapping my fingers on the desk. "Is that really necessary?"

Ms. Mullins came around the desk, and for the first time in my life, I felt like a cornered canary, running from a cat. The woman was intimidating.

"Your son's actions wounded another student, and you want to ask me if punishment is necessary?" She questioned, raising a thin, black eyebrow.

"I'm not saying he shouldn't be punished, but taking him out of school isn't going to make anything better," I said, rubbing a hand over my face. "I mean, all it's going to do is teach him that doing something wrong means he gets to stay home, right?"

"Right," Cameron said, grinning. "I'm good with staying home."

Ms. Mullins sighed. "Cameron, you're a bright young man and really I hate to see you wasting your potential on meaningless pranks and fights. Please think about your actions and go wait in the front office while I chat with your father."

"I think—" my son began, a calculating look on his face.

"Go," the principal told him, her tone dismissing any argument he may have had.

Cameron sighed, trudging out of the office with his bookbag tow. I watched him go and then stared after him as he went to go sit down. How had my son become so unruly?

"Alright, Mr. Wilson, Dr. Roland has a few points he would like to bring up with you," the principal told me, leaning over the desk menacingly. "Dr. Roland, say your piece."

"Well," the man said, clearing his throat, "Frankly, Mr. Wilson— can I call you Scott—?"

"Mr. Wilson is fine."

"Okay then. Mr. Wilson, I think Cameron is missing something in his life," the pale doctor said. He was wringing his hands and his face was going red. "I think he needs more."

"I agree," the principal said, nodding.

"Excuse me?" I asked her, sitting up. "My son has been given every chance in life, and he will continue to be given everything he needs to succeed."

She shrugged delicately. "I don't think so. *We* don't think so."

"It isn't about what you think," I said, waving a hand. "This isn't about opinions, yours or mine. This is about Cameron."

"Yes, and he needs something more in his life to be a well-balanced child," Ms. Mullins told me, unfazed by my attempts to change her mind.

"He needs a woman," Dr. Roland said quickly, blurting out the words.

"Um, what?" I asked, actually dumbfounded.

Ms. Mullins sighed, and I swore she rolled her eyes at her colleague.

"He means that maybe Cameron needs more of a feminine influence in his life, and perhaps someone who can spend time with him when you aren't able to," she said.

I dug my fingers into the armrest, frowning. "His mother isn't really in the picture.

"I'm well aware," she told me, and her harsh expression softened the tiniest amount. "Have you thought of hiring a nanny? Or some sort of service to look after him after school?"

"His grandmother sits with him after school," I told her. "It's not like he's alone."

Cameron had been taking the bus this year, now that my business had taken off full steam ahead. It was just me now though, and I could admit it was hard to juggle it all.

"Mr. Wilson, I'm afraid if something doesn't change, we will need to take drastic measures to ensure that the safety of the other students isn't put in jeopardy." The Doctor remained quiet as the principal's words sunk in fully.

I sighed. "So, he's suspended then?"

"Until further notice, yes," the principal nodded. "You can collect his classwork when you leave. The assistant in the front office is putting together his assignments now."

"He's ten years old," I said, rubbing a hand over my jaw. I really needed to shave. "Can't you cut him a break? Just this once?"

"This isn't his first offense, though this is the first time you've been here to pick him up," Ms. Mullins said, and she was looking down at me. I felt like a bug under a microscope.

"What do you mean?" I asked, raising an eyebrow.

"Your mother has been picking him up when he's in trouble," she said, "and I'm not surprised she didn't tell you about it. You haven't exactly been the most present parent."

Principal Mullins was not a woman who sugarcoated things. If she wanted to say something, she just went ahead and said it, regardless of what other people thought. I could grudgingly admire that about her. In my world, if you didn't speak up, you would never be heard.

"My business is very hectic," I told her calmly.

"Yes, I'm aware of what you do and how much time it takes away from your son," Dr. Roland said, seemingly finding his courage again. I forgot they made the kids talk to him and have therapy sessions every other week. I assumed he talked about me.

Of course the good doctor knew what I did for a living, though. I was sure the principal knew too. If she hadn't known, I would have been surprised. Mine was the most successful in the state. The oil business had always been notorious for its cutthroat nature, and when companies won out, they were well-known for it. It was the sort of business where competition was fierce and only the strongest survived to the end of the line. I always thought the saying "dog eat dog" perfectly covered the whole of the intense and ruthless work environment that existed within the industry that I had pretty much grown up in. To be able to succeed in the oil business, one had to constantly work hard to be at the top of their game. I could honestly say the market was highly volatile, with prices constantly fluctuating and the demand and need for oil constantly switching back and forth. Companies had to be able to stay ahead of the curve, changing to new technologies, rules of the game, and market trends. If my company failed to do so, we would left behind in what was essentially a race to the top, and we would struggle to keep up with competitors around us.

Manufacturers were continuously competing for market share and profitability in the intensely competitive market forces. They would use aggressive methods to win rich contracts, drilling rights, and important resources. For most companies, this frequently meant engaging in pricing wars, undercutting other competitors, and using political power to obtain an advantage that they may not have before. The stakes were high in the oil business, which was driven by massive profits. Companies committed large sums of money to drilling, exploration, and recovery in the expectation of finding oil and receiving large financial gains from whatever they actually managed to find. Still, the dangers in the oil business were enormous, as failed enterprises may result in large losses and even bankruptcy. Sometimes, I just didn't have time to be a doting, stay-at-home father. Things just didn't always work out that way.

The oil industry's dog-eat-dog mentality extended beyond company competitiveness, though. It also pertained to organizational internal dynamics. Employees were under continual pressure to perform, fulfill goals, and provide results for the business I was continuing to cultivate. Work could be extremely taxing, with extended working hours, levels, and the ongoing desire to show oneself. I inherited the company, but it was never something that was just given to me. Only those who could flourish in the demanding environment had a real chance at success. I was raised in that sort of environment. It was crucial to highlight, however, that not all parts of the oil industry were competitive. Collaboration and partnerships were very prevalent, particularly in large-scale initiatives that need substantial resources and experience. Companies like mine frequently created alliances to share risks, pool resources, and collaborate on complicated tasks. These cooperations usually resulted in beneficial results for everyone and helped to alleviate some of the risks. It was all on my shoulders. Though I had a team, the last call was always going to be mine.

No one understood the pressure I was under but me. I was the only one who knew.

Once, I might have thought it was too much to handle for me. Now though, I was glad I was thrown into the business just after high school like I was. It made me a stronger man and I was able to deal with much more stress now that I was used to it. I had gone back and forth on whether to toss my son into the mix. Maybe he was too young or maybe it would just be what he needed to push him into a better headspace. I couldn't figure out why he was acting out and I wondered why my mother hadn't told me she had to pick him up. She didn't like the business I was in either. My father had been a soft and easygoing man. He wasn't capable of taking the business on. The oil industry was a very competitive and ruthless one. Companies like mine had to always strive to remain at the top of the ladder, utilizing aggressive techniques and staying ahead of the curve, in order to survive and grow. it was necessary to survive. Only the strongest and most adaptive would be able to thrive in this environment, while those who couldn't keep up were left behind.

William C. Wilson, my great-grandfather, was not only successful in the oil business but also made substantial contributions to the sector through his innovation. His method of converting heavy oil into gasoline transformed the oil industry's efficiency and profitability, and it is a monument to his inventiveness and entrepreneurial zeal. The innovation of William C. Wilson had a significant influence on the industry. Before what he was able to discover, heavy oil was thought to be a waste product with little value. It was tough to improve and had few uses. However, he discovered a technique to transform heavy oil into gasoline, an extremely sought-after and profitable commodity, using his unique process. He lived a very long life and I was able to know him because of it. My own grandfather was just like him, like a carbon copy of the original.

William's invention not only created new opportunities for the oil business, but it also had profound implications for the world economy at large. I was told all about it constantly. I was raised on my great-grandfather's legacy. Because heavy oil could be converted into gasoline more effectively, more fuel could be generated from the same amount of resources, resulting in increased energy availability and lower consumer costs. I was proud to have such an innovator in my family line. What he did also helped to diversify the energy landscape and improve energy security by reducing the energy sector's reliance on conventional crude oil sources. The success of William C. Wilson in the oil industry was not solely due to his innovation. He was regarded for being a diligent and motivated man who was not afraid to take chances and embrace possibilities. He possessed a great business sense and was able to negotiate the industry's unpredictable and competitive character. He was a great man to look up to when I was growing up. When my own father was gardening and sitting in his armchair, my grandfather and great-grandfather were making a name for us to last the ages.

Despite the success he built into the Wilson empire, William C. Wilson maintained a sense of humility and always took time to share what he knew and learned with others, especially his family. I remembered him as a tough man with an easy heart for his family. He would frequently take the time to educate me on the ins and outs of the business world, offering significant lessons and insights that I still remember to this day. William C. Wilson's ingenuity and success in the oil sector were enough to inspire and impact the industry. His creative approach and entrepreneurial spirit served as an emphasis of the significance of pushing limits, accepting change, and always looking for fresh solutions to problems. His achievements have permanent imprints on the oil business and left our family as a powerful household name. That was the legacy that I wanted my son to foster in his everyday life. I tried so hard because I wanted him to have everything he needed to succeed.

"My work is important," I said to them both, standing up and smoothing down my shirt. "I'm sure you both take pride in what you do as well."

"That may very well be, but your son is desperately in need of something and you need to figure out what that something is before it's too late for him," Ms. Mullins told me.

"Actually, my fiance is going to be spending some time with him and helping him with classwork and such. She's going to act as a nanny until we can find someone else."

I didn't know why the words came tumbling out of my mouth. They were completely untrue. I didn't have a fiance or a nanny to show for my lies. How unconvenient.

Dr. Roland squinted at me. "Cameron has never mentioned you having a girlfriend."

"Well, I guess you don't know your students as well as you thought you did," I told him with a shrug.

I did feel guilty when he looked away, obviously shamed, but I couldn't stop now.

"Wonderful news," Principal Mullins said with a knowing smile, trying to derail my optimistic web of lies. "When can we meet her?"

Chapter 2

Daisy

"I'm about to be homeless."

"What are you talking about, Daisy?" The dark-haired woman sitting across from me said, her mug paused at her lips. "Are you having a breakdown or something?"

Penny looked at me like I was going insane. I sat across from my best friend at our usual spot in the cozy coffee shop downtown, and yet I didn't feel the usual amount of warmth and peace. My chest felt as tight as my wallet, and knowing that I probably didn't even have enough money to cover our coffee was making me feel sick. The scent of freshly brewed, dark roast coffee filled the air, mixing and mingling with the soft back-and-forth chatter of other people sitting at the booths. The cafe was a place where the two of us often sought a port in the storm, a familiar refuge from the chaos of our daily lives. Today, however, I couldn't escape the weight of the news I had received earlier that morning. It was like a punch to the gut and I didn't even want to be in the fight in the first place.

I took a deep breath, trying to steady my racing heart, and looked into Penny's kind, hazel eyes. She had always been such a good friend to me. She was a good listener too. If there was anyone who would understand, it would be Penny Sullivan.

"I don't even want to say it out loud," I said, pressing my fingers into my eyes. It was spring and bright outside the window to my right, but my hands felt cold when I let them drop to rest on the table.

"You can tell me anything," Penny said easily. She reached out, patting my hand. "Drink your coffee. You'll feel better. You know we both depend on our caffeine."

I managed a small smile, nodding. I tried to swallow and there was a lump in my throat.

"I found an eviction notice on my door this morning," I confessed to her, my voice barely above a soft little whisper. The words hung heavy in the air between us, and I watched as her face seemed to crumple with concern for me.

"What? Are you kidding me? That's absolutely ridiculous!" Penny cried, her voice filled with genuine worry. She threw her hands up. "How exactly did this happen? Have you spoken to your landlord? I'll go talk to him right now."

"No, Pen, please," I said, jolting up to grab her arm as she stood, dark hair flying.

She sat back down with me, her eyes bright. "Why? Did you talk to him already?"

I nodded, my eyes welling up with tears. I hated feeling so vulnerable and I hated even telling someone what my problems were. I was really bad at asking for help, and I always felt like I was a burden on anyone who had to deal with my problems with me.

"I called him right away, but he pretty much told me that there's nothing he can do about it. The building is being sold, and the new owners said they want everyone out of the apartments within a month. I don't know what to do. I have no idea what I'm supposed to do. I just— I can't afford to find a new place so quickly. I don't have the funds."

Penny reached her arm across the table, putting her hand on top of mine comfortingly.

"I could ask my dad for a loan for you," she offered, her face pinched like she already knew the answer.

I shook my head. "I know your dad is well off, but I can't do that. I don't want to be in debt to anyone."

Penny's dad worked on some big-shot oil guy's team and he saw more money in a week than I did in a month. Freelancing was a hard gig and it was tough to make a life.

"I already knew what you were going to say, but I had to try," Penny said with a sad smile.

"No, I really appreciated it, but I just can't," I told her.

"We'll figure this out, okay? No matter what you think, you're not alone in this," Penny told me. "We'll find a solution together. Everything is going to be okay. You'll see."

Her words made me feel a little flicker of hope, and I wiped away a hot tear that streaked down my cheek. Somehow, Penny always made me feel so much better. She made me feel like there was some kind of hope in whatever situation we were in. Maybe it was because she had been given everything she needed in life, but she truly believed that everything worked out in the end. It didn't matter how dire things were.

"Do you have any ideas?" I asked my best friend with a sigh. "Honestly, I'm open to anything at this point. Give me your wildest suggestion and I'll think it over. Go ahead, Pen, I know you have something kicking around in your head."

Penny's eyes were bright with serious determination as she leaned back in her side of the booth, contemplating what I had asked of her. I knew she would have an idea.

"Well, have you ever thought about being a nanny or something like that? You're really good with kids. Do you remember my cousin's birthday party?" Penny said, glowing with happiness at her own suggestion. "My nannies were always really stuffy and mean. I would have loved to have one like you, and it could be a good way to earn some extra money while you figure out where you're going to be living. What do you think?"

Once, what felt like a lifetime ago, I wanted to be a teacher. Then the one who believed in me most passed away, and all I wanted to do was be like her and keep her memory alive. I had pushed the teacher thoughts to the side and made room for my new dreams. I pondered her suggestion, and the idea slowly took root in my mind.

"You know, something like that might just work for me. I've always loved children, you know, and it could be a fulfilling job, right?" I asked her, but then my doubts caught up with me and I felt myself sinking. "But how do I even start? Won't it take too long?"

Penny's face lit up with excitement. "No way! Let's go ahead and make some fliers! We can go to the library and use their computers and printers, right? They have that, don't they?"

"Yeah, they have that," I told her with a slight laugh. "Don't you have stuff to do though, at the boutique?"

She waved her hand. "I'll just be closed today. It's totally fine."

"That's really sweet," I told my friend, reaching across to squeeze her hand. It wasn't like she needed the money from the sales, but the boutique her dad helped her open was important to her and it was the thought that counted.

"We'll come up with something pretty and smart, and then you can put them out around town. We can stick them up everywhere. There are definitely families out there who would love to have you as their nanny and I can probably make a few calls," Penny said, looking excited as she stood, sliding out of the booth.

"You don't have to do that. You're already helping enough." My words were true, but the real, deep truth was that I didn't want to have to nanny for some overly rich, spoiled child who had a million demands. I didn't need that kind of stress. The last thing I needed was some loaded, entitled set of parents constantly on my case.

"We'll figure it out," Penny said, sounding unconcerned by my conflicted thoughts.

A sense of relief washed over me as I realized I wasn't completely alone in this awful situation and I wasn't going to be any time soon. My best friend's unfailing support gave me the strength I needed to face whatever was ahead. I just needed to get a client.

"Thank you, really," I told Penny. "I don't know what I would do without you, Pen. If you're still fine to go, we can head to the library right away and get started on those fliers like you said."

We gathered our belongings, leaving behind our half-empty coffee cups, and made our way to the sidewalk.

"Get in the Benz," Penny told me, nodding at her fancy car. "I know you just walked from your apartment. We'll drive to the library."

Normally, I might have taken her up on that offer, but I needed the walk to calm down and clear my head. I liked walking anyway, and I was used to it after so long.

"Let's walk instead," I told her. "It's a few blocks and we can go to the Sunflower Co-op after to hang up some fliers."

Penny sighed, but she was smiling. "You and your exercise."

We walked together, hustling down the sidewalk in the bright, morning sunshine. The library was a big, red brick building. It was ancient and I loved it. It was peaceful and I used to spend a lot of my time inside when I was a kid. Once my dad retired from teaching and moved across the state, I wasn't there as often as I once had been. When I chose to stay where my mom grew up, I threw myself into making her proud and a lot of things fell to the wayside. As we entered the quiet, cozy space, the scent of dusty old books covered us in a familiar smell, providing a sense of comfort for me. We settled down at a computer. Penny's fingers flew across the keyboard as she designed the perfect flier, making it bright and colorful, like something that kids would be drawn to.

"But don't we want the adults to be the ones drawn to it?" I asked her, watching as she added a splash of neon orange and then hot pink.

"The kids will force their parents to hire you," Penny said brightly. "They won't have a choice."

"Nice," I said with a snort.

Finally, she hit the print button on the old computer, and the sound of the printer filled the big room. Penny grinned at me as the stack began to overflow. Holding the square pack of freshly printed fliers in my hands, I couldn't help but let myself begin to feel a new sense of hope for the future.

"How far is the co-op?" Penny asked, squinting in the sun.

"Just up there," I said, pointing across the green center of town, where the small park was.

I forgot that she usually shopped at higher-end places. The co-op was like something out of a European film, all covered in ivy and flanked by tall trees. There were bouquets of flowers on tall shelves outside, and fresh fruit and vegetables displayed in crates in the shade. Inside, the place was like a movie set. I absolutely loved it. It was one of the few places that had been renovated for a more modern look, or demolished altogether to make room for the rich oil men that seemed to be taking over my small hometown in droves.

As Penny and I made our way through the town park, the warm kiss of the sun pressed across our skin, haloing a golden glow over the scene around us. The vibrant hues of the flowers in full, spring bloom and the laughter of children playing on the swing sets filled the air around us, creating a peaceful and serene feeling. It felt like it was the best sort of setting for a heart-to-heart kind of talk with my best friend, and I knew I would be able to trust and confide in Penny about my recent life problems.

The two of us had been close friends since we were kids, though we had never been in the same tax bracket, and Penny had always been my biggest and most excited cheerleader. She had a stone-solid belief in me, even when I couldn't help but doubt myself. Today, I found that I needed her support more than ever. I had been having so many bad weeks, but this one really took the cake. I took a deep breath, deciding it was time to tell her my little secret.

"Hey, so," I began after a moment of silent steps from us both, my voice shaky with a mix of sadness and determination, "I've been going to a few casting calls for modeling jobs lately. Remember I told you I wanted to start and I got those headshots done."

Penny's round eyes widened with surprise, her smile spreading over her face. "Are you serious right now, Daisy? That's incredible! Why didn't you tell me when you found out? I'm guessing it wasn't today."

A wave of self-doubt washed over me, making my voice tremble slightly.

"Well, the truth is, I was just embarrassed," I told her, clearing my throat.

"About what?" Penny asked me, and I could feel her watching me.

"I know it's dumb, but it's just that I've been turned down every single time. I can't get any jobs," I told her, sighing so hard that it made my chest hurt. "It's been really hard to deal with, to say the least. I've been starting to think about whether or not I'm cut out for this sort of thing at all. I'm still not even sure."

Penny's eyes blazed. "Daisy, don't you dare give up on this. I know it's important to you. You have so much beauty it's insane. You're the prettiest person I know. Those casting directors just don't know what they're missing." Her face softened, and she knocked her shoulder gently into mine as we walked.

I sighed, but I did feel a little bit better. "But, I don't know, it's been so disappointing. Every time I get rejected feels like a personal blow. Maybe I'm just not meant to be a model, you know?"

Penny's gaze sparkled with determination as she looked at me intently from my side. We were still walking and I counted my steps, trying not to get too sad about the casting thing. It did feel like I should have been doing something else. I had never told her I wanted to be a teacher, not even when we were kids. I kept it to myself and close to my chest. It hadn't mattered in the end anyway.

"Daisy, remember when we were kids and we used to play dress-up? You were always the star of the show. You had this natural grace and elegance that captivated everyone. That hasn't changed. You were born to be in front of the camera."

I couldn't help but laugh at that. Her words hit a chord deep within me, pulling up long-forgotten memories of our carefree days of make-believe in her dad's big, richly furnished townhouse. I couldn't help but smile at the thought of us as little kids, so innocent to the sadness and stress of the world. My best friend had a way of reminding me of who I really was, even when I wasn't even sure of it myself.

"I don't know. What if I keep getting rejected by the directors? What if I'm just not good enough to be a model?" I asked my best friend, my voice colored with uncertainty.

Penny's expression twisted into something serious, her eyes filled with that same unwavering belief in me.

"You can't just give up, failure is a part of life. It happens to everyone. Failure is how we grow and learn to be better. You can't just let a few setbacks define you as a person," she told me, watching the kids as they went back and forth on the swings. "You have to remember that every 'no' brings you two or three steps closer to a real 'yes.' You have to keep trying and keep pushing for what you want."

"Thanks for saying that," I said, and a real warmth was growing within me.

"No, I'm not just being nice," Penny said, shaking her head in frustration. "Do you remember when I opened my boutique? My parents wanted me to go to school, but you believed in me and it made them believe in me too."

My steps halted for a moment and her words struck a chord deep within me, lighting up the flickering flame of determination that had been dulled by the eviction notice and everything else that was going wrong. I realized that giving up would mean letting my fear of losing win, and I didn't want to let fear take over my dreams.

With a new strength of will, I looked at my best friend and nodded. "Yeah, I know you're right. I can't let a few let-downs put me out. I'm going to keep trying, keep pushing forward, and I'm going to prove to myself that I have what it takes to make it. This nanny thing is the first step."

"Yes, I'm so proud of you," Penny said as she beamed at me with perfect teeth, her belief in me shining brightly. "That's the spirit and

I'll be right here by your side, cheering you on every single step of the way. That's what best friends are for, you know."

"And I have the best one," I said with a grin, throwing my arm around her as we walked.

We continued our walk through the park, nearly to the edge where the sidewalk met the grass. The heavy weight of my previous failures had already begun to lift and lighten. It was nice to have at least one person to care about what I did or didn't do. I didn't have a lot of that in my life. Penny's forever encouragement and belief in me, I knew I could find the strength to face any challenge that might lay ahead. I just needed one voice to tell me that I could do it. I didn't want to be held back by fear that I couldn't achieve what I wanted to. It was important to me and I needed to figure out a way to achieve my dreams.

It wasn't like it was just some side gig for me or like I wanted fame and fortune, Being a cover model wasn't just a career choice for me. It meant a lot to me to be able to fill the emotional void that had been left in my chest after all I had been through. After two failed relationships with men who didn't even appreciate me and then what happened with my mom, being a model became a crucial part of my path toward self-discovery and healing from what I couldn't even explain. After going through heartbreak and disappointment, I just wanted to find some sort of \ solace in the world of fashion and cover modeling. It was a place where I could change myself into something better, and where my worth was mine to control. I had to work for it, but I believed that I could do it. The photoshoots I had done became my place of peace, a sanctuary where I could feel fulfilled and showcase my inner strength and ability to overcome anything and everything. I had done a few small campaigns so far, but nothing majorly profitable.

When I stepped into a photo room with the shoot all set up, I would feel a surge of confidence and empowerment. The camera flashes illuminated my path, guiding me toward a newfound sense of self-worth. Each picture that was taken of me was a step towards reclaiming my identity and proving to myself that I was more than the sum of my failed relationships and hardships. Through being a cover model, I was slowly starting to find the beauty within me that had been overshadowed by the emotional turmoil I had been through. The industry was one that surprisingly embraced the things that made me unique, celebrating my little flaws and imperfections as part of my character. The first one I ever went to, they actually acentuated the freckles across my nose. My mom had always pointed them out, tapping each one with her finger. It gave me hope that I was doing the right thing.

Beyond all the glamour and glitter, modeling provided me with a platform to motivate those who had also experienced grief and self-doubt. That's what I kept thinking anyway, that I could help others once I gained traction. I wanted to be an example to them that they, too, could rise above the hardships they were experiencing and discover their own path to acceptance of themselves. Throughout my journey, I hoped to be a light of hope for others, reminding them that their value is not dictated by the judgments of others. Modeling, or at least the possibility of it, was quickly becoming my issue and also my therapy. It helped me to change my problems into something positive if I could, turning them into fire for my desire and determination. I felt a sense of fulfillment that nothing else could ever bring with each successful picture session or small show. Being a cover model was about more than simple outward validation and a luxurious sort of lifestyle. I didn't even want any of that anyway. It was about rediscovering my self-worth, accepting who I was even without my mom around to tell me, and motivating others to do the same if it all worked out. It was about replacing that emotional emptiness in my chest with self-love, self-acceptance, and the awareness that, regardless of what others think, I was always going to be enough. I couldn't give up on myself, not yet.

"There it is," Penny said, pointing up ahead. "There's the store."

For some reason, I felt like this was the beginning of everything.

Chapter 3

Scott

I was about to hire a nanny.

I walked briskly from the small parking lot to the bustling co-op in my small town, feeling a mix of hesitance and determination. Today was the day I had decided to put up a job offer for someone to look after Cameron. As a single father trying to balance work and taking care of my son in the state he was in, I knew I needed some help. The thought of entrusting someone else with the well-being of my kid was both daunting and entirely necessary. I stood out on the sidewalk and recalled meeting with my mom earlier when I stopped my son off to spend what was supposed to be a school day with her.

I pulled up in my sleek, black car to my mom's house, the familiar white picket fence and blooming, colorful flower beds greeting me as I parked off to the side of the street. The vehicle was a stark contrast to the picturesque, charming little house, though it had always felt too small to me. The sun was shining and it was mid-afternoon. If he wasn't in so much trouble for doing what he did, it would have been the perfect time to drop off my son for his visit with his grandma, but it felt wrong to have him here during what was meant to be school hours. As I turned off the engine, I couldn't help but feel a sense of unease. I really needed to have a chat with my mom. She had some explaining to do.

I got out of the driver's side, making my way around to open the door for my son. I ruffled his dark hair. He looked so much like my own dad that it was painful to look at him sometimes. I reached down and opened the door, stepping back to stand on the grass. Cameron hopped out of the car, his backpack slung over his shoulder, a mischievous smile playing on his lips. I gave him a look, reminding him he was in trouble. He wasn't at his grandma's for fun, it was a necessity until I could figure it out.

"Thanks for the ride, Dad," he said, his voice filled with excitement. "I can't wait to spend the day with Grandma."

"You need to remember why you're here, Cam," I said with a frown, admonishing him.

"I do remember," he said, obviously trying to school his face into something more guilty. "I just love spending time with Grandma. I thought you wanted me to be happy, Dad,"

I shook my head, smiling ruefully. The kid really knew how to pull all of the right strings.

I gave him a small smile, trying to hide my growing concern. "Have fun, buddy. You be good for Grandma, okay? I don't want to hear that you haven't listened to her."

My son nodded happily, his eyes shining with anticipation. "Yeah, I promise, Dad. See you later!"

"You have to remember to get all of your work done too," I called after him, but he was already far ahead of me. I rubbed a hand over my face with a sigh.

As Cameron bounded happily up the front steps of the house, I took a deep breath and made my way to the glass-paned teal front door. My mom greeted me with a warm hug, squeezing me tightly, her eyes twinkling with love and knowing. Her silver hair was under a gardening vi-

sor and her plump cheeks were pink. Helen Wilson was one of the kindest people in town. She was well-known for her canned, pickled carrots and her big, bright smile. She was the last woman my grandfather would have wanted my dad to marry, but they suited each other perfectly. They were both soft, easy-going people, not meant for the corporate world. Neither one of them had any interest in it anyway.

"Scott, my love, it's so good to see you," she told me, her voice filled with genuine happiness. "It's such a shame that Cam was suspended. I was sorry to hear it. He can stay here as long as he likes."

I didn't plan on making my mom babysit my son while he was on school suspension. This was just for the day, but it was nice that she offered. She really was a kind woman.

Hugging her back, I couldn't help but let my concern creep into my tone. "Mom, I think we really need to talk. This is very important and I'm confused about something. Why didn't you tell me that Cameron had been getting into trouble at school lately? They told me you've been picking him up early because of it."

My mother's bright smile seemed to falter for a moment, and a flicker of guilt crossed her pretty, lined face. "Oh, my dear Scott, I didn't think you had the time to hear it. I don't mean that in a nasty way, but you've just been so busy with work lately. I didn't want to burden you with it. I'm sure this will pass. He's a good boy."

I couldn't help but sigh, my frustration mixing with my concern. I understood that she had the best intentions. I knew that she always did, but sometimes, that wasn't enough. Cameron needed to be disciplined and to learn that constantly failing wasn't going to get him anywhere. You had to be the best to get the best out of life. I didn't want my son constantly getting in trouble at school and giving himself a troublemaking title.

"Mom, I may be busy with work but I'm still his father," I told her gently. I took a deep breath as a cool breeze blew across the plant-covered porch. *"I just really need to know what's going on in his life, especially if he's having trouble at school. I need to know."*

My mom nodded, her expression softening. "I understand that, Scott, and I'm so sorry that I didn't tell you. I should have told you what happened. Cameron has been acting out quite a bit, but I wasn't sure if it was a big deal. He's been getting into some trouble with his teachers. I wouldn't say it's anything serious, not until now, just some childish fun and some talking back. But I thought I could handle it on my own. I didn't want to have to bother you with it."

I ran a hand through my hair, a mix of emotions swirling inside of me. Of course I understood what she was saying. She was my mother and she was a good lady. She was all about taking care of the people around her and I loved that about her, but thinking like that sometimes got in the way of the truth and what was right.

"This serious stuff," I told her, and she gave me a motherly look of affection.

"Scott, honey, you're so grumpy," she said, reaching out to pat my cheeks.

"Mom, I'm a grown man," I said, shaking my head. *"I appreciate that you want to protect me from all of this, but I need to be involved in Cameron's life. He's my son. Me and you, we're a team now, and we need to tackle these challenges together, right?"*

My mother's eyes gleamed, and her voice was filled with a regret that I hated to hear. "You're right, my love. I'm so sorry about that. I should have trusted you more and I know you can figure out how to deal with this along with your work. I'll make sure to keep you informed about everything from now on."

I nodded at her, feeling very grateful for her understanding. It was nice to have some help with Cameron and I was so glad to have her around. We might have been two very different people with different ideals, but we could at least come together about her grandson.

"Thank you, Mom," I said, giving her a small smile.

"There it is," she told me, looking warm and happy. "There's that smile. When you smile you look so much like your father. You are your great-grandfather's and your grandfather's twin, but not when you smile."

"I know you never got along with either of them," I said, and she just smiled sadly.

"We had very different ideas of what a good life should be," she said, nodding. "That's okay. Sometimes people don't always mix the way they should."

"You and Dad were great together," I said, and it was the only thing I could really say. It was the truth.

My mom reached out and squeezed my hand as I heard Cameron watching tv inside, her touch comforting and reassuring. When I was a kid, I knew I could always turn to her for support. She was that same loving woman with my son. She was the rock that held us all together.

"I know you're a good father, Scott. We'll both make sure he learns from his mistakes and grows into a responsible young man, just like you did," she said. "Now, have you thought about what you're going to do? Cameron is perfectly fine staying here, but I do teach those gardening classes three days a week."

I rubbed a hand over my face. "The principal and the counselor had very strong ideas about how I should deal with Cameron's issues. They think he needs more of a strong influence in his life, someone other than you or me."

"And what did you decide?" She asked me. "More to the point, do you want some tea? You look like someone who could use a cup of tea right now."

I couldn't help but laugh. "Uh, yes to the tea," I told her. "And I think I'm going to hire a nanny."

With my stack of job advertisements in hand, I made my way to the community bulletin board right outside the grocery store. As I reached up to pin the first one to the big corkboard that already had dozens of announcements, my hand reached out and ran right into another person's, causing my fliers to scatter in the air like confetti at a party. She must have had some in her arms too and they went everywhere, falling around us and gathering on the concrete. I looked up with a furrowed brow to see a woman with long, bright blonde hair and a bemused sort of smile on her face. Her chocolate brown eyes sparkled with a mix of what looked like annoyance and amusement. She must have been half my age, and she was wearing a floral blouse with cut-off denim shorts.

"Wow, you should watch where you're going," she told me, her light voice laced with a hint of sarcasm. "You might knock into someone and spill their fliers or something."

I couldn't help but feel a slight a twitch of irritation at the tone of her voice. "Maybe you should just watch where you're going too," I retorted, letting my own annoyance seeping into my voice. "What if I had a coffee? You would've spilled it everywhere."

"Coffee sounds nice," she said, grinning. "I might get one later."

"Good for you," I muttered. She was the kind of person where you couldn't tell if they were upset or not, or they were just kidding. I hated not having control of the conversation.

That being said, she was ridiculously pretty and it was hard to ignore. Both of us bent down and crouched on the concrete outside the door to gather all of the fliers, our hands brushing against each other as we scrambled to collect them before the people going in and out could step on them. At that moment, I couldn't help but notice how soft her touch felt against my own hands. Her hands were thin and tanned, her fingers delicate and elegant. What I felt right then was an odd mix of attraction and irritation, a strange cocktail of feelings that left me feeling slightly off-kilter as I looked at her.

The door opened and a dark-haired woman in expensive-looking clothes and shoes stepped out, her mouth already open.

"Daisy, they said it was fine to put them up inside too— oh, hey there," she said, looking at the blonde woman and then at me.

"Hey, Penny, this is, uh," the woman whose name must have been Daisy said, looking at me.

"Scott Wilson," Penny said, nodding. "My dad works for him."

I didn't recognize her, but then again, I didn't know a lot of the people who worked under me. I had a lot of employees and judging by the way she was dressed, her family wasn't neglected by the company. I just nodded at her, looking back to Daisy immediately.

"I'm Daisy Gray," she said, giving me a slight smile. Once we had managed to get all the fliers in hand, she gave me a few of mine with a flourish. "Here, I think these ones are yours. Mine are brighter."

I took them from her, offering a half-hearted smile that felt more like a frown. "Thanks. Yours look like Skittles ads."

Daisy laughed and it made my heart twist. "Yeah, Penny said the color would help me get the job. I'm a little skeptical."

Penny said something, but I wasn't listening. She went back inside the store, but something about Daisy was keeping me there. My curious side got the better of me, and I happened to glance down at one of the bright, colorful fliers in my hand. It was an ad for a nanny, and I thought about what a crazy coincidence it was to run into her. As I read my way through the details of the flier, I couldn't help but feel a small glimpse of hope. Maybe this was fate's way of pushing me in the right direction and it wouldn't be as difficult as I thought to find someone to look after Cameron.

I looked up at the woman still crouched in front of me, whose name I now knew was Daisy and found her watching me intently the same way I had been watching her before. There was a small glimpse of vulnerability in her dark eyes, a hint of something more beneath her smooth exterior. She was waiting for me to say something to her.

"Are you a nanny?" I asked her, my tone filled with both surprise and relief.

I couldn't believe my luck.

She nodded. "Yeah, I guess I am. I'm looking for a new job. Why do you ask?"

I hesitated for a moment, pointing to the flier in my hand. "I'm actually looking for a nanny for my kid," I told her, feeling an odd mix of embarrassment and hopefulness. "I came here to put up these ad fliers to try and find someone. I didn't think I would so soon."

Daisy's eyes widened, and a genuine smile spread across her face.

"Well, isn't that crazy and convenient? It looks like fate brought us together, Mr. Wilson," Daisy said, and I could see something new and bright in her eyes too. It looked like hope.

"You can call me Scott," I told her, rubbing a hand across my neck.

"And you can call me Daisy because that's my name," she said, shaking my hand.

I couldn't help but chuckle at her words, feeling a weight lift off my shoulders, though I wasn't sure that the two of us would get along. Maybe this chance encounter in town was more than just an explosion of fliers all over the ground. Yeah, Daisy wasn't exactly my favorite person, but there was something about her that drew me to her personality.

"Look, I have a couple of things to do beforehand, but what if I take you to dinner tonight?" I asked her as we stood up. "We can discuss the details and you can sign the contract."

"Contract?" She asked me, brows furrowed.

I nodded. "We'll chat about it later. Meet me at Dinero's around 7:00?"

Daisy agreed and I could feel her watching me as I left the co-op behind.

Dinero's was a quaint Italian restaurant nestled in the very heart of our little city. As I entered the dimly lit restaurant with its candles flickering on every table, I spotted Daisy waiting by the entrance, her bright, sunny blonde hair catching the soft glow of the overhead lights she stood under. She wore a soft-looking pink sundress that put her curves on full display, and her brown eyes sparkled with anticipation. My heart thumped hard in my chest and I hadn't felt this way in a very long time. I pushed the feeling down.

"Hey there, Daisy," I greeted her with a polite smile. "I apologize for being a few minutes late. I dropped off some takeout at my mother's house where my son is tonight."

I hadn't told my mom I was meeting with a potential new nanny, just that I had a business meeting to go to. She was more than happy to let Cameron stay the night.

Daisy returned the smile, her lips turned up mischievously.

She said, "Scott, fancy seeing you here, huh?"

"Let's go get a table," I told her, clearing my throat.

We were escorted by a hostess to a cozy little corner table, the flickering candlelight casting a romantic sort of ambiance over the entire affair. Maybe I should have chosen somewhere more formal for our business meeting. As we settled into our seats, the waiter approached the table, ready to take our drink orders for the night.

"Oh, what a lovely couple you two make," she said, all but cooing at us. "How long have you been together?"

Daisy's cheeks went red. "Oh, we're not—"

"My fiancé and I will have the special for tonight," I said, giving her the menus back. I swallowed hard, trying to keep a straight face while I could feel Diasy staring at me.

"So," she said, dragging out the word after the waitress had left, "when did we get engaged? I think I would have remembered since I just met you today, but maybe I blacked out or something."

I scrubbed a hand over my face. Instead of answering her, I dug around in my briefcase, pulling out a stack of freshly printed papers, still smelling hot from the printer. I put a pen on top of them, sliding it all across the table to her. She looked down, confused.

"That's the other thing about this job," I told her, looking her in the eyes, straight on. "I need you to play a part for me. I'll pay you double whatever your rate is, but I need this to work out for my son. His future education depends on it."

"Okay," she said, dragging that out too. "What part is it that you need me to play?"

"Well, Daisy Gray," I said, letting out a breath. "I need you to be my future wife."

Chapter 4

Daisy

"Are you ready for this?" Penny asked me, her voice breaking me out of my thoughts.

I nodded. "I need this job, Pen."

"That's not what I asked," my best friend said, giving me a worried look.

The Mercedes Benz smelled strongly of leather and of the cherry-scented fragrance tag hanging from the rearview mirror. I wiped my sweaty hands on my jeans and looked over at her. Her mouth was flat and she looked more serious than I had ever seen her.

"What's with that face?" I asked her, watching her.

Penny sighed. "Scott Wilson is a hard sell, Daisy. Do you know what I mean? My dad works for the guy and he pretty much hates him. He's all work and no play."

"Well, I'm going to be working for him, so that's fine with me," I told her with a shrug.

I hadn't told her that Scott Wilson was paying me to pretend to be his new fiancé so that his son's teachers would think he was a good dad. I assumed that was why anyway. He told me that his son, Cameron, had been suspended from school and his teachers said something about him needing more time with people who would care for him. Something about a woman's influence. It was strange to me but I wasn't about to question it when the man was going to pay me double and also move me into his spare room to be able to watch out for his son.

It also helped that Scott was the most handsome man I had ever seen in my life.

"Just be careful," Penny said, still looking worried. "He's not a great guy."

"Maybe we just don't know him well enough," I said, but I would have normally taken Penny's thoughts to heart. I just really needed the job.

"He's the head of a huge oil company and his profits are through the roof," Penny said, pointing. "I mean, look at that house. It's bigger than both of my dad's houses put together."

'I'm sure his ego is bigger than both your dad's houses put together too," I said, and she shook her head, grinning. "I'll be okay, Pen. I'll make sure to check in with you once I'm all settled inside the house."

"You better," she warned. "Are you sure you don't want me to help you? I can carry a bag or two."

"I only have two bags," I said with a small laugh. "See you later, Pen. Thanks for the ride."

I nervously took the steps out of the expensive car and looked up at the ridiculously large, modern-looking house in front of me. I had never seen a place as big as this one. There must have been at least ten rooms inside. The house was gray and the windows were large. It wasn't a place I would assume a child would like to grow up in. Inside, I could see the place lit up by soft lamps and overhead lights. I knew that the interior would be all minimalist furniture and décor. I hated that kind of thing. It was the exact opposite of how I grew up, surrounded by my dad's knick-knacks. I took a deep breath as I went up to the big, dark wooden doors. This was it, my very first afternoon on the job as little Cameron's nanny. I took a deep breath and grabbed my two overnight bags, ready to face whatever might lay ahead once I went inside of the house.

The door opened before I could even grab the handle or think to knock

"Daisy," he said, his sky-blue eyes watching me with interest. The sun lit up the dark waves of his hair that were struck through with silver, and I swallowed hard.

"I'm here," I said, feeling very childish and unprofessional already. "Ta-da," I said weakly.

"You are. Did you have any trouble finding the place?" Scott asked me politely.

He came out of the house fully to greet me, smelling of intoxicating, woodsy cologne. The man had a stern expression on his face, and I wasn't sure how to talk to him. He definitely wasn't the most welcoming or friendly person and Penny's opinions of him rang through my ears. I wasn't sure how to approach the situation. What was I supposed to say? Was I supposed to act like his girlfriend now or just when we were around the appropriate people? He gruffly motioned for me to follow him inside the house, and I obediently trailed behind him, shuffling my bags inside.

"I'll get those," he said, motioning to the overnight duffles. "Here, hand them over."

I nodded, though he moved by me too quickly for me to even say thank you to him. We both went inside the house, and I looked around in surprise. The interior of the house was actually warm and cozy, painted in reds and browns. The couches in the enormous living room were covered in knitted throws and there were bookshelves in every room, full of books of every kind. Immediately, I felt safe in the space. Scott led me up the stairs to what must of been one of many spare bedrooms. It was where I would be staying while I was Cameron's nanny. Scott told me he needed me for the duration of his son's suspension from school and he didn't say if or how long he might need me after that. He was silent for most of the walk up the stairs and to the room, and I could feel the tension between us beginning to grow bigger and more taut with every step. It was obvious that he was not happy about having a nanny in his house, but I knew that he needed me just as much as I needed him. We would both deal with it the best we could.

Once we reached the room, Scott dumped my bags unceremoniously on the floor.

"Wow, thanks," I said, unable to keep the sarcasm from my voice. "The hospitality here is immaculate."

"Go ahead and make yourself at home," he muttered, before turning to leave the room. I couldn't help but feel a little pang of painful disappointment at his lack of warmth for me, but I should have expected it. "I'll be downstairs and you can meet Cameron when you come down."

I spent the next few minutes unpacking and settling into my new room. It was cozy, with a large window that overlooked the backyard. The yard had a huge treehouse, but it looked brand new and never used. There was a tire swing that didn't seem touched.

"I would have killed for a tire swing like that when I was a kid," I said to myself.

I steeled myself and looked in the antique mirror on top of the dresser, psyching myself up to go downstairs and meet the kid I was about to spend most of my days with. My footsteps sounded like lead down the wooden stairs, though they had rug runners.

"Are you Sunflower?"

I nearly jumped out of my skin as a kid who was almost as tall as I was burst out from behind the banister of the stairs, grinning widely at me. He looked a lot like his dad.

"Am I what?" I asked, almost laughing.

"He's a big jokester," Scott said, appearing from out of what must have been the study. "Don't mind him. Cameron, say hello to Daisy. I told you she's going to be your nanny."

"I didn't want a nanny," he said, squinting at me. "Are you going to make me clean my room?"

I leaned down, grinning. "I'm going to make you do your homework *and* clean your room. After that, we'll have ice cream and watch movies. How does that sound?"

Cameron, who was frowning, shot me a huge grin, wrapping his arms around me in a big hug.

"I guess that's a yes on the nanny debacle then," Scott said, letting a surprised little chuckle out.

"I like you, Sunflower," Cameron said, nodding at his dad.

"Daisy," I corrected, giving him a wink, though "Sunflower" was growing on me.

"Now, it's not going to be all fun and games," Scott admonished his son. "Daisy is here to look after you and make sure you do your work the way you're supposed to. You're suspended son, it's not a vacation from school."

"I know, Dad," Cameron said, pushing his face into something more serious. "I promise I'll take it seriously."

"We'll make sure he gets through this with a smile on his face," I said, nodding at him.

"Yeah, we'll see," Scott said flippantly, and my good mood sunk once again.

I tried to gather myself and attempted to focus on the positive aspects of the job. It was good pay and Cameron seemed like a good kid, despite his issues, and I was going to try really hard to make a good impression on him. At least he seemed to like me right away, unlike his dad. His father seemed annoyed by my very presence most of all.

"I'm going to head up and put my things away," I said, giving them both a quick smile.

I hurried back onto the stairs and ran quickly up to the landing, finding my auburn colored room with ease. I settled into the cozy room in the big house, my new home for the next few weeks. I still couldn't get over how cottage and library-like the interior of the house was when compared to the outside. I wasn't complaining though. I wished that Scott was the kind of man who wasn't too grumpy to answer normal, everyday questions. There was only so much optimism that I could muster in one go. The walls were adorned with portraits of who I assumed were relatives of Scott and Cameron. There was a stern, unpleasant-looking man hanging over the fake fireplace that I really did not like the look of. The air was filled with the comforting scent of freshly brewed coffee and I wondered idly if Scott was going to get some work done in that office. Was I supposed to watch Cameron now? I didn't think so. I had just finished unpacking my bags and decided to call Penny to share the latest update on my new job. She was probably itching with curiosity by now anyway.

When the phone began to ring, I sat down on the big, comfy bed. This job was only for a few weeks until I got enough money to find a place to live and fund my modeling starts, but it was a nice room and I really liked it.

"Hello?" Penny answered the phone on the third ring, her tone filled with interest. "Daisy, how's the new job going? Have you settled in yet? How is the kid?"

I grinned, feeling a sense of familiarity and warmth for my friend.

"Slow down," I said, laughing a little. "The house is absolutely beautiful, nothing like it looks on the outside. Cameron, the little boy I'm looking after, is such a sweetheart. He's a troublemaker, but he's got a good heart, I think. Scott is a different story."

"Ooh, yes, spill it. What is he like?" Penny's high voice grew eager and bright, and I swore I could almost see her leaning in closer to the phone in her apartment. "Is he like I said he would be?"

I hesitated for a moment and then I managed to take a deep breath. I was trying to find the right words to describe the stern, no-nonsense man downstairs. Compared to the bright little boy down there, Scott was like a storm cloud ready to turn into a tsunami.

"Well, he's kind of a challenge, if I'm being honest," I said, twirling a lock of hair around my finger. "He's obviously really successful. He always seems busy and preoccupied with work. He's super stern. I think he's still just trying to get used to having a nanny in the house with them."

Penny's voice was filled with concern. "Oh no, are you serious? Is he giving you a hard time? I can come to talk to him."

"He's your dad's boss, Pen, you can't talk to him," I said with a small laugh, trying to lighten the mood a little. "He's not giving me a hard time, but I guess it doesn't matter anyway. I'm not here for him, and he's not exactly thrilled about having me here. It's like he's not sure of my abilities or something like that. I'm not going to let it get to me."

"You're being really positive," Penny said as she let out a slight sigh of relief. "You sound like your old self, before the eviction notice. Yeah, that's the spirit, Daisy. I'm so proud of you and I'm sure Scott will come around once he sees how great you are with little Cameron. You know you can win anyone over."

"I don't know if that's true," I said with a sigh. "I couldn't win the landlord over."

"No one could have done that," Penny said softly.

I smiled to myself, so happy for Penny always being there for me when I needed her.

"Thanks for being there for me, Pen. I really needed to hear that. But you know what? Whatever Scott tries to pretend to be, I think there's something more to him. Maybe he's more than I think he is. Maybe under that tough skin, there's a caring father who just wants the best for his son. I think that's why he's doing this."

Her voice went soft. "You've always tried to find the good in everyone. You know, I do admire that about you. Just be careful and don't get too involved. Give it some time, and I'm sure Scott will come to see all the teaching and care you're going to show his son."

I nodded, even though Penny couldn't see me. She was usually right about these sorts of things. Being around her father's business associates had gotten her used to men like Scott, and she would know more than I would. I could only hope for the best.

"Yeah, you're probably right and I am being careful here," I told her. "I'm going to keep Scott at arm's length and just keep my attention where it's supposed to be. Everything is going to be fine."

There was nothing else to do but that. It would be a little hard to keep him at arm's length if I was pretending to be the woman he was in love with. I wasn't even sure how we were going to get Cameron to play along. Maybe we wouldn't need him to. I decided to keep that little secret to myself because though I had signed the contract, I wasn't even sure what it meant for me. I felt a little silly even thinking about telling Penny I was going to do it.

"See? This is going to work out for you, Daisy," my best friend told me. "You've always had a way with people and you know that. Just keep being who you are, and I'm sure everything will be okay. If that guy gives you any trouble, let me know. Boss or not, he'll be getting an earful from me."

I couldn't help but laugh. "You're such a good friend, Pen. I'll keep you updated on how things go with Scott and Cameron. Once this is all over, we can try to find me a new apartment and maybe I can work on my cover shots. Who knows, maybe Scott will end up becoming a good friend."

"See? You always see the best," Penny laughed, her voice filled with a familiar sort of knowing. "Anything is possible, I guess. Just remember, you're working there for the little boy, and he's what really matters. The rest will fall into place once it needs to."

I hung up the phone and took a deep breath before letting it out again.

There was a knock at the bedroom door and I stood up, opening it.

"My dad wants to know what you want for dinner," Cameron said, standing there with a big, excited grin on his face. "He said it's up to you tonight."

"That's very sweet of him," I told him, and it was true. It made me feel warm to think of it. "Can you tell him I want to cook for you guys, though? I want to cook a whole dinner."

Cameron nodded, taking off barefoot down the hallway. Scott hadn't told me what the kid did to land him in school suspension, but I was sure it couldn't have been anything too bad. He was a sweet kid, though I could see that he had a mischievous streak.

"Dinner huh?" Scott asked as I walked downstairs a little later. He looked at me, his gaze traveling over my jeans, t-shirt, and cardigan. I felt myself blush. He said, "Can you cook?"

"I'll guess you'll find out," I said, shrugging.

"What do you need?" Scott asked me, and I followed him into the kitchen. "I'll get the grocer to deliver the supplies here in an hour or so."

"An hour?" I asked, my eyes going wide. And to think I was going to take the bus. "Wow, okay. I can make you a list then. Thank you."

He just nodded, disappearing down the hall and getting on a phone call. He really was such a busy guy. For some reason, I couldn't get those bright blue eyes out of my head.

Later that evening, I had everything I needed to make dinner for all of us. I wanted to show them that I was capable and responsible and that Scott didn't make a mistake when he hired me the same day he met me. I set the pot on to boil and start cutting up cheese to go with the bread. Cameron was sitting at the counter in the humongous kitchen, watching me as I puttered around getting things together for the dinner.

"Why doesn't your dad have staff?" I asked him, watching him eat apple slices after I cut the fruit and handed them over.

His brow crumpled. "I thought you wanted to cook. You said you did."

"I do want to cook. Usually, houses like this one have a full staff though," I said, wondering if I was being too nosy and pushing ahead anyway. "Do you know what I mean?"

He nodded. "Dad gets us takeout. We have a maid, but she only comes when we're not here. Dad likes to have the house to ourselves ever since Mom left us behind."

I stopped dead, blinking. I knew I shouldn't ask and it wasn't my business. I let it go.

"So, are you hungry?" I asked him, smiling.

"Uh," he said, pointing behind me, "is that supposed to be doing that?"

I turned quickly to see that the soup had caught flame and was blazing high. I felt my eyes go saucer-side. Panic quickly set in, and I rushed to the stove, only to find that the flames were still burning high. The smoke alarm blared loudly, filling the house with its shrill sound. I grabbed the pot without thinking, pulling it away from the heat, and my hand stung sharply as the metal burned me. I heard Cameron sound panicked behind me.

"I'm getting Dad!"

Scott stormed into the kitchen, his face red with displeasure. "What on earth is going on?" he shouted to the place at large, clearly angry with being interrupted.

I stuttered an apology, feeling hot tears burning in my eyes, and my hand started throbbing with pain. I had already messed up on my first day and it had been such a hard week for me. I had been trying so hard to be positive, but I was ready to break down in tears. Seeing my distress, little Cameron came running into the kitchen.

"Dad, it's okay! Daisy tried her best and she did good," he told his father, defending me. I looked at him with a small nod, touched by his kindness.

There was a long time with me holding my fingers, feeling pathetic, and Scott sighed. He reached up over the fridge and turned off the alarm, and then he looked at me.

"Your hand," he said, coming over to me. He was so tall and he towered over me. I smelled his warm cologne. He bent to look at my fingers, taking my hand with surprising tenderness. "It's not too bad."

"I didn't mean to burn the food," I said tightly, trying to be strong and not cry.

"I know," Scott said quietly. I looked up at him, swallowing hard, and his face looked soft and vulnerable for a moment. "Cam," he called over his shoulder. "Go grab the first aid kit from under the bathroom sink please."

I heard Cameron take off running, and Scott ushered me to sit at the counter. He went over and turned off the stove, putting everything to the side. He grabbed a kitchen towel and ran it under the water, coming back over to me once he was done. He spun my chair toward him, leaning over me to grab my hand.

"Here, grab my belt for support," he said, sounding kinder than he ever had before. "This may sting a little."

I nodded and he put my good hand on his leather belt at his hip, letting me hold it while he held my burned fingers. He gently pressed the cold, wet dish towel there and I bit my lip, feeling the pain burst over my skin. He looked up at me, giving me a small smile.

"Thank you, I can do it," I said, letting go of his belt and looking away with warm cheeks. I took the towel from him and focused on pressing the ice cold to the wound.

"Got it!" Cameron said, sliding into the room with an expensive-looking medical kit.

"This is burn cream," Scott told me, pulling out a little packet. "Let me do it for you."

Without waiting for my response, he came back over and took my hand again. I looked up at him, watching how intently he was focused on helping me, and I tried not to smile. So there was something soft underneath that hard exterior. Maybe it was all an act.

"Try not to burn yourself again," he said gruffly once he was done, shattering my last thought of him.

"I'll do my best," I said sourly. I pulled my hand away from him.

"I'm still hungry," Cameron said, complaining, and I heard Scott sigh.

"Yeah, okay," he grumbled. "We'll just go out for dinner instead."

He grabbed his car keys and motioned for us to follow him out to the black Range Rover parked outside. He had four cars parked by the drive, and I knew they were all his. I didn't even have *one* car, let alone a car, and then a few more vehicles to spare.

"I want eggs," Cameron said, and Scott glanced at him in the rearview mirror as he drove, nodding.

It felt strange to sit in the passenger seat with him, but it was a good kind of strange. It was the kind of strange that a girl could get used to in the long run. I held my hand.

"Does it hurt?" Scott asked, staring at the road ahead.

"It's okay now," I told him. I shifted in my seat. "I can't believe I burned tomato soup."

"Is that what you were making? Tomato soup and grilled cheese?" He asked, and a small laugh left his lips.

"Yes, actually," I said and I couldn't help but laugh as well.

We eventually ended up at a nearby diner, and Cameron jumped out. I stopped him, making him grab my good hand to cross the seat. Scott opened the door for us and we sat in a booth to order our meals. The atmosphere was a little tense, but I struck up a conversation with Cameron, asking him about his favorite things to do and his hobbies. I just really wanted to get to know who he was and how he had come to need someone to look after him. A smile crept onto his face, and I knew that we were starting to bond.

"Dad, what time is the history fair?" Cameron asked suddenly, digging into his ketchup eggs. "Ms. Mullins said I could still go if you take me."

Scott paused with his spoon at his mouth, and I could tell he had no idea what his son was talking about. He looked at Cameron and then at me. Though I didn't know anything about it either, I decided to help him out.

"Your dad actually just told me about that," I said, pointing my fork at him and grinning. "He's really excited to take you, but you need to tell him the time. You never said."

"Oh, right," Scott said, quickly agreeing with me. "We're both going to take you."

Scott gave me a *look* and my heart went wild. Time to be his future wife.

Chapter 5
Scott

My mother was staring at me like I had dirt all over my face.

"Cameron, my little love, why don't you go and find us a good movie?" She said, waving a hand over her shoulder at my son.

Cameron nodded excitedly, hurrying out of the small kitchen to the cozy sitting room.

"Mom, it's not as out there as it sounds," I told her, holding up my hands in surrender. "Daisy agreed to it. She's going to be the nanny."

"I signed a contract," Daisy said quietly, nodding.

"You signed a contract," she responded, still sounding unconvinced.

I took a deep breath as I sat at the table in my childhood home, the familiar scent of my mother's perfume had greeted me at the door, as soon as I went inside. This was not how I had envisioned spending my Saturday afternoon, but desperate times called for desperate measures and I needed someone to know. Daisy was by my side, her nerves obviously as frayed as mine were. My mother had been waiting for us in the sitting room, her expression a mix of interest and concern. It had been a last-minute visit and my mom seemed surprised to see us. I glanced over at Daisy, silently urging her to take the lead in the situation. My mother had been looking at her, watching her carefully. She was a kind woman, but she was wary of anything that might damage her family. Daisy straightened her shoulders and began to talk, her voice smooth but filled with anxiety.

"Um, Mrs. Wilson. I just wanted to thank you for seeing us on such short notice," Daisy said, her voice still a hint of polite formality. For some reason, I didn't like it. I wanted her to be familiar with my mother and I wanted them to know each other.

I wanted to speak, but my mom was the one person who made me hesitate to say whatever I wanted to say. She was the one person I didn't want to disappoint other than my son. Now that my grandfather and my great-grandfather were gone, that is.

My mom nodded, gesturing at the top of the stove. "Of course, dear. I'll make some tea. What is this all about? You're Cameron's new nanny? You both seem so very serious about this. Of course, my boy here is always too serious for his own good," she said as she grinned over her shoulder, putting the kettle on the stove top.

Daisy gave her a weak smile, and I could see how nervous she really was.

I sat forward and cleared my throat, suddenly aware of how strange and ridiculous this situation would sound to my mother. I rubbed my hands over my face, letting out a sigh.

"Mom, we need to talk to you about something important and it's not just the nanny thing," I said and then I stopped, searching for the right words to explain myself to her. I didn't want my mom to look at me like a loser or something who couldn't get a woman without a contract. "You already know how much I care about my son's education, don't you? It's too important to let it fall to the wayside."

A look of understanding crossed my mother's face. "Well, yes, Scott, of course. I know how important it is to you, especially after what happened this week. What does that have to do with anything?"

"It's complicated," Daisy said, shaking her head as she wrung her hands.

I looked over at her, sitting beside me at the kitchen table where I had spent a lot of my days as a kid. She was golden in the midday sunlight, glowing bright and beautiful. I shook myself, trying to turn my thoughts to the matter at hand that we were explaining. I took a deep breath, preparing to reveal our absurd plan to my mother in full.

"Well, lately, you know his teachers have been raising concerns about my commitment and my responsibility as a parent to Cameron," I told her. She crossed her arms where she stood, nodding and listening to me intently. "They pretty much said that they believe that I need to find myself a stable relationship to show them that I'm capable of providing a nurturing environment for my boy, or that's how I took it anyway. That's where Daisy here comes in."

My mom looked unsure as she turned her eyes to Daisy. "You're involved with this too?"

Daisy nodded, and her hands were squeezed tightly in her lap, her fingers twitching.

"Yes, Mrs. Wilson. Scott needed a nanny and he put this on the table for me to decide, and after thinking a lot about it, I told him I would help him with his problem," Daisy said, talking very quickly to get it all out in one go, I assumed.

"The contract you were talking about," my mother said. The kettle went off and I saw Daisy jump out of the corner of my eye. My mom filled the teapot with hot water and put bags in the mugs waiting on the table. She looked up after pouring the water, a mix of surprise and worry etched on her face. "And what exactly does this plan call for?"

I took a deep breath, and my heart was pounding in my chest just like it was when I told my mom that I wanted to go into business with my grandfather instead of her and my dad. "Well, Mom, Daisy has agreed to pretend to be my fiancée for the foreseeable future. We thought that by presenting ourselves as a committed couple to the staff at the school, it would pretty much curve the teachers' doubts about my ability to provide a stable home for Cameron."

Mom's eyes narrowed as she thought over our words. "Honey, do you think this is the right way? Lying is never a great foundation for anything, especially Cameron's future."

"Mrs. Wilson—" Daisy began, her words sounding rushed and shaky.

I put my hand on Daisy's, silently reassuring her, and she looked surprised. Her brown eyes were wide and bright, and she was staring at my mouth before looking back to meet my gaze. I felt my chest stirring with warmth and I looked away, letting go of her hand. I could feel my mom staring at us and I heard Cameron's movie playing loudly.

"Mom, I understand where you're coming from, but I really wanted to prove to the teachers that I was responsible. A little lie to help both Cameron and me is nothing in the long run. I just wanted the best for my son, and if this was what it took, then I was willing to do it." I was watching my mom after my statement was out there, waiting to see how reacted.

There was a small moment of silence as my mother seemed to think over our words. She sipped her tea, adding sugar and milk from the cannisters on the table. I did the same, but Daisy took hers just black. Finally, my mom sighed and looked at me with a mix of affection and also genuine worry. I hated seeing that look on her familiar face.

"Scott, my love, I just want you to understand that I support you in wanting the best for your son, my grandson. But you have to remember that honesty and decency should always be your guiding principles. Cameron looks up to you. What does he think about all of this?"

"He said he would play the part," Daisy piped up, holding her tea like her hands were cold, though the temperature in the house was pleasant. "I think he believes it's all a game or something."

My mother sighed. "I don't know that all of this is what's best for him."

"I get what you're saying, Mom," I told her, nodding. I sat forward, staring at her. "It's either this or Cameron gets expelled from school. The school here in our little town is the best in the district. I couldn't take the chance."

Helen smiled softly, her eyes filled with some sort of sadness. "Did you ever consider just cutting back your hours at the office? You could work from home."

"Realistically, the company needs me in the actual office," I told her, wincing. "I'm the face of the business, Mom. You know that."

"I know all about that," she told me, nodding. "I was glad when your father chose to open the plant nursery with me instead of taking over the business like your grandfather wanted him to."

I had heard it all before. I knew what my mom thought of the oil business. I already knew how much she wished I had been like my dad. He never understood me though. They were perfect for each other and when he passed, a part of her did too.

"I know that, Mom," I said easily, keeping my voice soft and even.

"I think I'll go take Cameron for a walk and we'll have a little chat about this," she said, giving us both a strained smile. "I want to make sure he understands."

"You don't have to do that," I told her. I felt both guilty and relieved though.

"Oh, Gregory Carmen and his wife are churning peach ice cream today and they invited me over to try a scoop or two," she said, already heading into the sitting room. "Cameron loves peaches. We'll just be an hour or so and we'll see you two later. Daisy, it was nice to meet you, darling."

Daisy nodded, giving her a weak little wave. The two of them left through the back door.

After a long moment of heavy silence, Daisy and I shared a semi-relieved glance, knowing that despite the ridiculous plan I had hatched up, we seemed to have my mother's understanding and support for the moment. The house was quiet but for the ticking of the clock over the fridge and the movie still playing in the sitting room. I was thinking about how my mother hadn't mentioned the age difference Daisy and I, though I knew it didn't matter anyway. It wasn't real and she had no reason to care about age.

"Your dad was a gardener," Daisy said finally.

I nodded, smiling faintly. "A horticulturist. That's what he liked to be called. He met my mom at the city's Fall Fair. He had the best sunflowers in the state." A thought came to my mind and I looked at her, smiling. "That's what Cameron called you. Sunflower. It fits."

"And Daisy doesn't?" She asked me lightly, turning toward me so that her knees brushed mine under the table.

"It does, but you're warm—yellow like a sunflower," I told her. She looked at me, her cheeks going pink, and I realized what I was saying and cleared my throat. "Uh, anyway, he died a few years back, right after Cameron was born."

"Oh, I'm so sorry, Scott," she said quietly, reaching out to squeeze my hand and then letting go again. She looked away, shifting in her chair and looking as if she wanted to say something. "My mom passed not that long ago. My dad moved away afterward. They were divorced but he always loved her, I think."

"Were you close to her?" I asked, itching to know more about what made Daisy Gray who she was.

"Not as much as I would have liked to be," she admitted. "She traveled around a lot and I stayed here with my dad. He worked at the library for years and years. I'm trying to be close to her now though, even though I know I can't really make up for lost time."

"Yeah, I wish I had spent more time with my dad even though we never had very much in common. He didn't really care about making money or anything like that. That kind of stuff wasn't important to him," I told her. I didn't know why I was admitting my life story to this woman, but it was spilling out of me like it had just been waiting to have the time alone with her. "I don't want Cameron to ever lack anything and I work as hard as I can to give him the best out of this life. That includes you now, I guess."

She smiled slightly, nodding. She looked pleased with my assessment of her. She seemed to think about everything I said and she finally answered my statement.

"You're more like your grandfather than your dad, I'm assuming," Daisy said wisely.

"If I had been more like him, maybe I wouldn't be in this mess to begin with," I said, letting out a long breath. "He was always a big believer in the little things, but my grandfather looked at the bg picture, and I liked that thought better. Now I'm questioning it."

Daisy looked sad. "You don't know what you really have until you don't anymore."

"He kept my room the same as the day I left to live my grandfather when I was fourteen," I told her, nodding. "Do you want to see it?"

She perked up, nodding. I stood from the table and she followed me down the hallway that branched off from the kitchen. It was the last room on the left.

"Oh," I said as I stepped inside for the first time in months. "I guess Cameron has been staying in my old bed when he comes over." The thought made me feel warm.

"You really liked fishing, huh," Daisy said, stepping carefully inside. There was a small smile on her face when she looked over her shoulder. "You're just a small-town kid at heart. I knew it."

I sat down on my bed, looking around as Daisy inspected the place, standing on her tip-toes to look at books and magazines on the shelves. There was no dust on anything and I knew my mom had always kept the room pristine, but it looked like Cameron had been reading my old comic books. I was happy to know it and also wistful for the carefree moments in my childhood when I could just read on my bed with no stressors. As I sat in the quiet peace of my childhood bedroom, tons of memories began to flood through my mind, instantly reminding me of the unfailing support my mother had always given me. From the time I was a little kid, she had been my biggest supporter, pushing me to reach for whatever it was that would make me happy and to never settle for less. Now, as an adult facing a hard situation, I couldn't help but think back on the loyalty and love she had continued to show me throughout the years. Even after it was obvious that my father's side never really accepted her, she continued to let me see my grandfather and learn from him.

I leaned back against the familiar comfort of my bed, watching Daisy as she moved around. The sunlight streaming in through the window and casting a warm glow on the room, making Daisy's yellow hair glow. The walls were covered with pictures of plants l and petrified specimens that I were pressed in paper over the years, each one a reminder of the person I could have been. Maybe at one time, I did want to be like my dad. My eyes fell on a photo of my mom and me, taken on my graduation day from high school. Her smile was radiating pride and joy, and I knew my dad had taken that picture. I hadn't said a word to him all night, but he didn't care. He was just as proud of me as anyone, no matter how I had turned out.

Thinking back on that moment in time, I couldn't help but smile. I was thinking of Cameron's graduation and who all would be there to cheer him on. The smile was broken by the knowledge that I was making my son lie, and my own father would have never done that. He wasn't ashamed of anything about his life. What kind of dad did that make me?

"What is it?" Daisy asked me. "You're looking very contemplative over there."

I looked up to find her staring at me, sitting in my old computer chair, though the computer had been traded for my son's tablet.

"I'm wondering if this is right," I admitted to her.

Daisy sat down next to me. "What? You're just doing what you have to do for your son."

"Maybe," I said, shaking my head. "I'm asking him to lie for me, though, at his own history fair. I just don't know if I'm doing the right thing."

"Hey, you worry too much," Daisy said softly, her hand brushing mine on the bed. I glanced over and she smiled, making my heart ache at how lovely she was. "Cameron adores you. I've only known you guys for a little while, but even I can see that."

I was taken by Daisy as I had never been with another woman. Even Cameron's mom didn't enchant me the way that Daisy Gray did without even trying.

"We should head back downstairs," I told her, standing up quickly. It was too warm and safe there with her, sitting side by side, and I needed to get some distance. "My mom and Cam will be back soon enough."

Was it my imagination or did she look disappointed? It had to be all in my head.

"Okay, sure," she said, looking away. "Uh, actually, can I ask you something?"

"Yeah, anything," I said, my hand on the doorknob.

"I wanted to know if I could have half of the day off tomorrow? I have something I need to do," she said, twirling her hair like she did when she was nervous or unsure. I had noticed that about her. "I know you said weekends are usually off days for me, but I just wanted to make sure."

"That should be fine," I said, nodding at her. "It's a Sunday, but remember the history fair is tomorrow and I need you there."

"I'll be there. I'll make it to the history fair," she told me. "But what I need to do is important. I have to do this for my mom."

Chapter 6

Daisy

The city spread out around me, a huge landscape of glittering buildings.

"Second Street drop off!" The bus driver called out, and my heart was racing with excitement.

"Well, don't you look pretty," a gray-haired woman said as I went down the aisle. "Good luck in there."

I smiled at her, nodding. Everyone knew why I and the three other girls on the bus were getting dropped off where we were. There was a long line outside the refurbished warehouse, nearly wrapping down the sidewalk, but I wasn't going to let it deter me. I had brushed and curled my long hair to perfection and did my natural makeup perfectly, accentuating my almond-shaped eyes and my round, full lips most of all.

"Thank you," I told her, smiling and feeling like a million bucks as I left the steps of the bus.

The sun was shining down on me, bright and never-ending. My phone was buzzing in my pocket.

"How far was it?" Penny asked me when I answered. "Have you gone in yet? What did they say? I bet you got it."

I couldn't help but laugh. I was in a great mood and I had a good feeling about today. Penny had offered to drive me, but I liked the silence of the bus ride. I liked to have the time to think.

"It was two hours away," I told her, making my way to the end of the line. "I just got here, Pen. There are so many other girls here and they're so pretty."

Was that doubt starting to sneak in? I tried to push it down and not glance at the glittering, gorgeous girls in line who were all vying for the same cover model position.

"You're going to knock them dead," Penny told me, her voice bright.

"I'll talk to you later," I told her quickly. She needed to get back to the boutique anyway.

I made my way into the casting call with a combination of enthusiasm and apprehension. As models, photographers, and casting directors socialized and prepared for the auditions, the room was alive with excitement. I took a deep breath and reminded myself to stay perfectly calm and pay close attention. This was my big break, my chance to be a cover model in a real advertisement in the big city. I had to keep a calm head and think about what was at stake. This was serious for me and I wanted to succeed. I needed this and I needed to prove to myself I could do it.

A polite attendant gave me a number to pin to my shirt and she pointed me to the lounge as I made my way over to the registration desk. I took a seat among a bunch of other prospective hopefuls, and each of them had a distinct mix of confidence and anxiety. We were all hoping to make it in this world. We swapped encouraging nods and smiles quietly understanding the shared dream that had brought us all together. I couldn't help but feel so very afraid. I wondered what Scott and Cameron were doing. I wondered if they were having fun. Some small part of me wished I was still there at the house, helping Cameron grow and learn, but this was something I needed to do.

My number was soon called by the stiff-looking announcer by the door, and I made my way to the audition area. It was barren and cold-looking, and I felt immediately exposed as I brought my headshots over to the table. The casting director for the cover model gig, a sharp-eyed woman holding a clipboard, welcomed me politely. She took little time scrutinizing my portfolio, her reviewing gaze scouring each page of my short career in pictures. I tried to keep my cool, reminding myself that I had planned for this particular occasion specifically. I tried to tell myself that this moment in time wouldn't and couldn't define me, but I really wanted this to be my big shot. I imagined making it in and being just like the woman I looked up to. I envisioned a lot of things while the panel of people looked over my pictures, and I made myself focus on the task at hand.

"Alright, Daisy," the casting director called out from the table where she and two other people sat, her sharp voice professional yet detached. "Come on up here and let's see what you've got. Show us your best here."

I walked onto the set with measured steps, the weight of the room's expectations bearing down on my shoulders like a leaden coat. The photographer, a seasoned expert with an eye for detail, stood with his camera and took me through many stances and poses where he began to snap pictures of me. I made an effort to find my inner confidence and emanate the appeal and attraction that I knew the camera was looking for and more importantly, what the judges were looking for.

I tried very hard to put my heart and soul into each gesture as the lights flashed around me and the camera snapped photos of me.

I felt at a little uncomfortable, and I tried to make myself act like a natural-born model poised to take over the business. I wondered if I would ever feel at home in the studio like my mother must have. The photographer's kind words of encouragement and the casting director's approval, nodding and waving at me, strengthened my desire to succeed. But just as quickly as it all had started, the whole thing was over. The casting director went ahead and thanked me for my time, her tone polite but distant.

I could sense the disappointment in her voice before she even uttered the words, "I'm sorry, Miss Gray, but you didn't get the front page. You were much too stiff. Better luck next time."

My heart sank and felt so heavy in my chest, and I struggled to hold back the barrage of tears that threatened to fall down my cheeks. I thought I was doing so well and It felt like a punch to the gut, a solid, crashing blow to my dreams of being a cover model. I thanked the casting director with a short nod and I left the room to hurry back onto the street, my head spinning with a horrible swirl of mixed emotions. I was too stiff in my shots? What did that even mean? I tried to control my thoughts, but I couldn't help but feel like a complete failure like I was just consistently falling short of the mark.

"Maybe next time," one of the other models said, and I wiped my tears, hurrying away.

As I walked to the bus station, the weight of my huge, hulking failures weighed heavily on my shoulders. I entered the air-conditioned bus, took a seat by the window, and gazed out of the foggy glass at the passing city and then the green, spring countryside. My thoughts were consumed by self-doubt and irritation at what I couldn't accomplish. I felt like other girls got their cover model jobs so easily, so why was it so hard for me? Why couldn't I ever seem to catch a break in my life?

What was I doing so wrong that I was constantly getting beat down by life?

The bus journey felt endless and forever, and each mile that passed by was a harsh reminder of my own mistakes. I didn't even want to call Penny and tell her what happened. It felt like she always had faith in me and I always let her down. I watched the city skyline fade into the distance behind me, desperately wishing for the opportunities that seemed to be just out of reach for me. the doubts that gnawed at my self-confidence, threatening to kill it, were overwhelming. I felt so heartsick and like such a failure.

But when the bus reached my hometown, I felt a spark of something burning within me. I was trying not to let this failure start to define me. I had traveled too far and fought way too hard to allow one rejection to break me. Maybe I would throw myself into helping Cameron and the modeling thing would figure itself out in time. I wiped my tears away with my fingers and straightened my back, trying very hard to convince myself that failure was just a stepping stone on the route to real success. I was going to take a page out of Penny's book and feel positive that I had even tried in the first place. It was still disappointing though and I didn't think I would be able to hide that once I stepped off of the bus.

I took a deep breath and then let it out again as I got off the bus, relishing in the comforting aroma of what had been my home for so long. The heaviness of disappointment just kept pushing and gnawing at me, but it no longer held me in the grips of sadness like a hostage.

I hurried off of the bus and back onto the sidewalk, trying to keep my head high. I picked up my phone to see if Penny would give me a ride back to Scott's mansion, but she didn't answer me. I tried twice before assuming that she was too busy at the boutique to come and pick me up. I didn't like being a burden to anyone anyway. I would rather walk than have to call anyone else. There was really no one else to call for me anyway. I walked a few blocks and stopped for a moment, feeling a little tired and downtrodden.

"Daisy?" Called a familiar voice, and I spun around.

He was in his Range Rover, dressed in a slick black suit, and looking at me curiously.

"Scott," I said, looking through his passenger-side window. "Where's Cameron?"

"Mom is at the house with him for an hour or so while I drop off some documents," he told me, gesturing at the big building to my left that must have been his company. "Are you walking home? Get in and I'll drive you."

"I can walk, it's not that far to your house," I told him, hitching my bag higher on my arm. "I need the time to think anyway."

"Daisy, it's a mile and a half," he said, nodding at the passenger seat. "Think in the a/c."

I nodded, finally deciding that he was my boss and it would be fine if he gave me a ride to what was essentially my work. Thinking about his success made my stomach sink. Would ever be successful? Scott had a thriving, rich company and he was the boss.

"Is there something wrong?" Scott asked as he drove, breaking me out of my thoughts.

"Uh, no, there's nothing," I lied, shifting in my seat. The car smelled like his cologne. "How's Cameron? Is he ready for the history fair?"

"You're changing the subject," he answered me bluntly. "Why is that?"

I let out a breath. "It's not a big deal, but I went to a casting call and I didn't get it. It's fine though, I didn't expect to get it anyway."

"I'm supposed to be the morose one, not you," Scott said, and I smiled faintly. He said, "Casting call, like for modeling? Or acting?"

"Cover modeling," I told him as I watched the city whoosh by my window.

"Well, I'm sorry you didn't get it," he told me. "Better luck next time though."

For some reason, that just made my blood boil. Scott wasn't a man who had probably ever had someone tell him that in his life, and it was annoying that he was pitying me.

"I don't need your pity," I told him, glancing away even though I felt him staring at me. "I could have walked home too and I didn't need the ride either."

"Excuse me for trying to help you," Scott said, his tone sharp.

"I've gotten by on my own long before you came along," I told him, and i knew I wasn't really making any sense, but I hated feeling so small and pitied.

Scott stopped the car, pulling over to park by some little electronic storefront shop.

"What are you doing?" I asked him. Looking at that handsome face was almost too much, but i managed to glance over. He was looking at me, all blue eyes, dark waves, and frown lines.

"I wasn't pitying you, Daisy," He told me earnestly. "I don't want to fight, but I am sorry you didn't get the modeling gig you wanted. I'm sure it was important to you."

That might have been the kindest he had ever sounded. I nodded at him and the look on his face made my eyes begin to burn. I tried to blink them away but it was too late.

"I'm sorry, just ignore me," I told him shakily, turning away.

He put a warm hand on my arm. "Hey, what is it? Did something else happen?"

"No," I shook my head, trying to keep my voice steady. "It's just that I'm doing this for my mom and I feel like I keep letting her down. She was a really successful cover model."

Scott was quiet for a moment but the heavy warmth of his hand was comforting to me.

He shook his head, sounding gruff. "Are you doing it for you or because you want to honor her? You shouldn't throw yourself into something just because you feel like you have to. You should do something that makes you happy instead of trying to live up to other people."

"You sound like you know a thing or two about that sort of thing," I said quietly, wiping my eyes. His hand slid from my arm to rub across his face and I missed the heat of it.

"Yeah, I know a little something about expectations and feeling like you need be something even if you want something else," he said, letting out a dry little laugh.

"What do you mean?" I asked him. I wondered if I was being too nosy.

Scott actually answered though, surprising me. "My dad wasn't like his dad and his grandfather. I was raised to be like them, though. I spent most of my time with them, and I think they wanted that. Sometimes, I wonder what my life would have been like if I spent more time with my own dad, but it doesn't matter much now."

I thought for a moment. "Your house doesn't fit the way it looks on the outside."

"What?" He asked, letting out a surprised chuckle.

"The outside looks like a wealthy businessman and the inside looks like a—" I began.

"Horticulturist?" Scott asked, grinning sadly. I nodded and he said, "Yeah, I know. It's funny how things work out."

We spent the rest of the car ride in comfortable silence and when we finally reached the house, I was happy to be there. I found that it felt like home to me already and it was a warm feeling, one I wasn't really used to. Scott's mom left, giving me a kind smile, and Cameron was bouncing around the house to get ready to go to the history fair.

Chapter 7

Scott

"Do you need a coat?" Scott asked me, standing and waiting at the door.

It was chill for spring, the weather cooling down once the sun had begun to set.

"Uh, sure," I said. I was wearing a short-sleeved top and jeans. "You don't have to though."

"I know," Scott said quietly, handing me the nice gray coat he was wearing and wrapping it around my shoulders.

He went to the hall closet and grabbed another one for himself and I tried not to smell the cologne on the one I was wearing. I felt warm and safe as we left the house for the school. We reached the gymnasium and Cameron was practically vibrating with energy.

"It's so cool!" He called out, and I grabbed his hand to stop him from running across the parking lot.

"Wait a minute," Scott said, grabbing his other hand. "Calm down, bud. We're here."

All of the students and their families were rushing around the school gymnasium, marveling at the many exhibitions and stagings. I stood at Cameron's side, examining the space for any intriguing displays that might capture his interest. His attention was all over the place. He grabbed my hand, his enthusiasm obvious in the way he was nearly bouncing up and down. He pointed to a stall displaying replicas of ancient Egyptian antiquities, and we let Cameron tug us along behind him. Scott looked tense, but he also looked happy to see his son so excited. I knew he was thinking about how we might have to play pretend and we never had before. I was trying not to feel too anxious about it. I could get through it.

"Look, Daisy! Dad! Can we go see that too?" Cameron asked me, his eyes wide with wonder as he saw a Viking exhibit where kids were gathering to watch a man make a straw doll. "That's so cool."

"Of course, Cam," I told him with a smile. "Let's go check it out. Scott?"

He nodded, a faint smile on his face as he followed behind us. I could feel his gaze.

"Go ahead and look," he told Cameron, letting him run off to the display.

"Thanks for letting me come with you guys," I said, my arm brushing his gently.

"I don't think Cameron would have forgiven me if you didn't," he said with a snort.

"Is that the only reason?" I asked him, feeling my heart pick up the pace.

He looked at me and I saw something soft and open on his face. Just as we reached the World War Two booth beside the Viking one that Cameron was at, Scott went stiff at my side. He was looking at something behind me and I could hear the click of high heels as someone approached us. I turned around, wondering what could make a man like Scott look like that.

"Good afternoon, Mr. Wilson," a stern-looking woman greeted us, her voice carrying a hint of polite formality. "I see you're enjoying the fair." She looked at me, raising a perfect eyebrow. "I don't believe we've met. I'm Principal Mullins."

"I'm Daisy Gray," I said, clearing my throat. What was I supposed to say? Maybe I should let Scott take the lead. "We're having a lot of fun. Thanks for letting Cam come."

Scott, ever the quick thinker, glanced at me and then back at the principal. "Yes, we are. Daisy here has been an amazing addition to our family. We're actually here on our first outing together as a family. Daisy is my fiancee. Remember I told you about her?"

I nodded, trying to look as convincing as I could and playing along with the charade.

"Yeah, we're so happy. I was disappointed to hear about Cameron, but he's a good boy," I said, turning a bright smile in Scott's son's direction. "He's going to be just fine and we're getting to spend a lot more time with him, so that's a plus."

Ms. Mullins's eyes went wide with surprise, but she maintained her professional composure. "Well, that's wonderful to hear. It's always great to see parents and guardians actively involved in their child's education, and I'm sure Cameron will fill me in on the details once he's back at school."

Scott and I shot each other a knowing glance, silently acknowledging the importance of this moment and how Ms. Mullins seemed to be happy enough to see Scott with me. I wondered for a moment what we looked like from an outsider's perspective. He was older than me, but I couldn't imagine anyone mentioning that to him or me. I wondered idly if I looked good standing by him. Did I fit there in the space at his side?

As Mr. Thompson moved on to greet other families, giving us a polite nod, Scott let out a long sigh of relief. I felt better now knowing that I was going to be fine playing pretend.

"That was nearly perfect," he whispered, his voice tinged with a mix of amusement and relief. "I think she bought it, don't you?"

I laughed softly, the tension leaving me. "I mean, we made a good team, didn't we?"

Scott nodded, his eyes filled with appreciation. "Yeah I think—"

He stopped, looking behind me, and I looked too. Cameron was chatting with another boy. He looked deep in conversation and by the end of it, they did a little handshake.

"Scott?" I asked him. "What's wrong? What's going on?"

"Cameron," Scott said instead, but he glanced over at me as his son approached. "Was that the boy that you got in a fight with?"

"You got in a fight?" I asked, surprised. I couldn't see little Cameron hitting anyone. "You shook hands with him."

Cameron nodded, his chin high and proud. "We made up. I said I was sorry."

"You did?" Scott asked. He looked surprised but pleased all the same.

"Daisy would have said she was sorry if she did something wrong," Cameron said happily, nodding at me. "I wanted to be like a sunflower. She's bright."

I felt my eyes well up and my smile was shaky as I reached out, taking his little hand.

"Thank you, Cam," I told him. "We're so proud of you."

Scott nodded. I looked at him and my breath caught. He looked like a man in love.

The weight of duty weighed heavily on my shoulders as I sat at the head of the long mahogany table. The seat was familiar to me and had become something of a second home for me. The room around me was filled with a quiet murmur of voices as my executive team analyzed the most recent reports and estimates for the coming days ahead. As the owner of an oil company, these meetings were routine, but there was a sense of enthusiasm in the air today. I watched the people around the table, wondering what I had missed in my absence. It was Tuesday and while we were all usually glued to our hot cups of strong coffee, there seemed to be more anticipation today.

My Vice President, Mark, cleared his throat and caught my attention. He was a portly man with a thick mustache and a serious expression. He had always been perfect for the job.

"Scott, I have something important to discuss with you and that's why the meeting has been called today," he said, his voice filled with an edge that I had never heard before.

I leaned forward, my interest truly piqued. "What is it then, Mark? Spit it out."

"We have an incredible opportunity to expand our operations to another city, a few hours away from here," he said with a smile. "Scott, I'm telling you, this is big. The potential for growth and financial success is enormous."

I was filled with both excitement and a heavy dread that I knew was going to gnaw at me. Expanding the business even further to a new city would surely benefit this company, but it would also mean spending lengthy amounts of time away from my son, even more than I already was. Iit had always been hard to strike a balance between my personal and professional lives, but this decision was about to tip the balance.

"Tell me more," I responded evenly, keeping my voice firm even in the midst of my conflicting feelings. I didn't want to let my personal thoughts get in the way of the expansion. This could be something absolutely amazing.

Mark reached down and grabbed a folder from his briefcase. He began organizing the information to present to me, and I was surprised he didn't already have everything in a neat and polished presentation. He must have been too excited about it to be as thorough as he normally was. He showed me everything. He was thrilled about the new market possibilities, the potential consumer base, and the strategic benefits of establishing an important presence in another city. The comments he made provided a vivid image of accomplishment and the possibilities of what it all could mean sparked my interest.

Out of the corner of my eye, I caught sight of the photo of Cameron on the background of my phone as it lit up with some random notification. My son's bright smile reminded me to keep in mind the special times we shared together, the baseball games we went to when he was younger, and goodnight stories I used to read to him. Lately, we hadn't been as close as we once were, but it had been hard for both of us to find a balance once his mom left him in the dust. My heart ached at the prospect of being separated from him for a long length of time, but I had to remember that the company was just as important.

I realized why I agreed to take over the business in the first place. I wanted to have it for Cameron's future and for mine, to give him some of the best chances in life. If spending some time in a new city meant ensuring that future, then maybe, just maybe, the sacrifice would be worth it in the end. Cameron would be able to understand. He was old enough to get it. I was doing it for him.

I inhaled deeply and stared at Mark, resolve in my voice. "Come on, Mark. Let's get started. Let's go ahead and get everything set up."

There was a mix of relief and excitement washed over Mark's face as he nodded in agreement. He was obviously very ready to be able to help make this a possibility. I knew, for him, it was an easy choice. He had made his career his only hobby. He didn't have a family or even a stable home to think about. He had one condo in the city and I knew he barely had any furniture in it, he traveled so much. It wasn't as easy for me.

"I knew you'd make the right decision, Scott," he told me, nodding as the other people in the room agreed. "I know this is going to be a game-changer for the company and for you too."

The remainder of the conversation in the meeting was spent looking over the expansion's logistics, periods of time, and the plan of action. Everyone in the room was buzzing with excitement as they began to imagine the possibilities that moving the business to another city would open up. We were clearly entering a new chapter, one that would test us and push us to our limits to the very edge. The people in the room with me weren't the kind of people who backed down from a challenge though, and knowing that made my resolve grow even stronger than before. As the conference eventually came to an end, I couldn't help but feel proud and hopeful about the future. Yes, being apart from Cameron would be difficult for both of us, but I knew this was the best decision for both him and the company at large. He had Daisy now and he wouldn't be alone. I tried not to think about Daisy Gray too much. Going down that road would make me question everything I was already set on. I was determined to make it work, to leave Cameron with a legacy he would be proud of.

I grabbed my stuff and exited the conference room with newfound gusto. The path ahead would be difficult, but I was prepared to meet it head-on if I had to. I thought that my grandfather would have been so proud. I couldn't help but grin as I made my way back to my office, knowing that my choice would determine not just the future of my company, but also the future of my kid and the life he lived because of it. As I sat in my office chair, I couldn't shake the thrill that was coursing through my veins after the meeting. The decision to expand to a new city had been taken, and it was now time to get down to business and do my best to make it a reality. I called for another meeting with my senior executives, including Mark, to discuss the next steps together. We gathered in my office and met once again, this time armed with a big board and a thick stack of notebooks and folders. The work day ended and I was pleased enough.

My mind was still racing with the specifics of the extension project when I went through my front door. As I walked into the foyer, I took out my phone and dialed Mark's assistant, Jessica's, number. When the phone began to ring out, I answered it with an exhausted but resolute sort of voice. I was excited but it had been a long day.

"Hey there, Jessica. It's Scott calling. I wanted to go over some of the details of the expansion and I know Mark is at dinner. Do you have a few minutes to jot some notes down for him to look at when he gets back?"

"Of course, Mr. Wilson. I'm here to help with anything. What do you want the notes to say?" Jessica told me, her voice filled with polite enthusiasm.

I wandered into the living room and sat down on the couch, my eyes looking around the room absentmindedly. "Well, we've finalized the location for the new branch, and I've been working on establishing partnerships with local businesses, you know. Mark needs to schedule a day when we can both go and check out the new city and where we want to begin construction. I want his input on the marketing strategy. I might be away for weeks once this thing is really going. I need to know if he's going to step up."

As I dived deep into the details of our conversation, I heard a creak from somewhere in the house. Cameron and Daisy were supposed to be upstairs finishing his schoolwork for the day and I knew they wouldn't be down until later. There was another creak.

Daisy entered the room and I couldn't help but stare at that golden blonde hair and her long, tanned legs. She was so beautiful and it was getting hard to ignore. I watched her and then looked away. She moved again though and she stood by the doorway, her arms crossed and a pinched expression on her pretty face.

"Scott," she said, her soft voice hard and tense.

"I'll let you get back to work Jessica," I said into the phone quickly, hanging up.

"What about Cameron? Have you thought about how this will affect him?" Daisy said without any lead-up to it, her voice tight with anger. She heard the conversation.

I looked up "Daisy, I didn't even realize you were down here. Look, I understand that this is a big decision, but Cameron is going to be able to understand. He knows that I'm doing this for his future and he has you now to help him. That's why you're here."

Daisy's face contorted with frustration and there was a little hurt there too.

"Scott, he's still just a kid. All he can see is that his dad is never around to help him. He obviously acts out because he's craving your attention. I can't believe you haven't noticed. You can't expect him to understand whatever the bigger picture is. To him, all that matters is you," Daisy said, waving her hands. Her cheeks were bright red.

"I know it's been tough, but this expansion is necessary for the growth of the company," I told her, trying to calm her down. "It will provide a set future for my son and I think he'll come to understand that."

Daisy shook her head, her eyes welling up with tears. "You keep saying that, but it doesn't matter. It's not just about the company, Scott, or about some ridiculous expansion. This whole thing about your relationship with your son. You can't keep prioritizing your work life over him. He needs you, don't you understand? He's a good kid and he deserves to have a parent who's really there for him."

Her words resonated within me and struck a nerve. For a moment, a sliver of gnawing doubt crept into the forefront of my mind. I wondered for a second whether or not I was making the right decision. I questioned if I was sacrificing too much of my son's childhood for the possibility of even more success. I already had a lot of success in my life, but this was different. Before I could even respond to her, Daisy turned on her heel and stormed out of the room, the sound of her light, angry footsteps echoing through the whole house.

"Daisy!" I called out, but there was no answer from her.

I stood there in the living room in silence, the weight of her words sinking into my consciousness. I realized that Daisy had so very easily touched upon a truth that I had been avoiding and she had pressed at it until it hurt and bled. My absence had indeed taken a toll on Cameron, and maybe it was time for me to reassess what mattered to me. Maybe. As I thought over the situation, the hard sound of the front door slamming shut echoed through the house. I knew that Daisy had left, angry and hurt. The realization hit me like a wave, and I felt a mix of regret and determination wash over me.

Chapter 8

Daisy

I stormed out of the house, the door slamming shut behind me. My heart was pounding, and my mind was clouded with anger. How could Scott not understand how important it was that Cameron had a stable influence in his life? We had just had a huge fight, and I couldn't bear to stay in that house any longer. So, I walked away. It wasn't my job to make sure Cameron was loved and fulfilled. That was his father's job and apparently, it wasn't that big of a deal for him. I walked the streets of the city, my stomping footsteps fueled by frustration and hurt. I wasn't even sure why it bothered me so much.

Maybe I just expected more from Scott and that's what hurt me. I should have known.

"Penny was right," I said to myself, wrapping my arms around my body in the cool night air. "I really do always try to see the good in people and maybe that's a bad thing."

I wandered aimlessly, the city lights blurred into a kaleidoscope of colors, and the sounds of traffic and people merged into a chaotic symphony. My mind was so preoccupied with my anger that I didn't even notice how far I had strayed from the familiar neighborhood where I worked. My frustration began to subside and I felt myself cooling down as my steps slowed down the sidewalk. There were fewer and fewer people as I walked further into the deep dark of the city. I had never been in this area before. I started to feel a little shock of anxiety as I kept my head down and hurried.

"Just keep walking," I told myself. "Just keep walking and everything will be fine."

I patted my pockets and I realized that in my emotional departure, I had forgotten my phone. I wanted to kick myself for acting the way I did. Why had I been so hasty? Something about Scott made me so emotional, whether those emotions were good or bad. I finally felt like I was getting somewhere with him and then he goes and pulls something like this. I felt empty when I thought about it and I just wanted to sleep. It was really too bad that I didn't know where I was. I eventually ended up in front of a little convenience store that I had never been to and never even noticed before. It was definitely a sketchy-looking place, but it was my only choice. I realized how it stupid it was for me to just leave like that. I knew I was confused and disoriented in this strange portion of the town. I decided to swallow my pride and ask for directions, sighing as I made to enter the store. The bell above the door chimed as I pulled open the creaking glass. I walked inside and looked around. The store was poorly lit, and the shelves were piled high with many different products, though I wasn't looking for anything. Behind the counter, a middle-aged man who smelled like burnt cheese was reading a crumpled newspaper. It was dark outside and my eyes adjusted to the difference in light, even though it wasn't bright. I went up to the man cautiously, my voice shaking as I asked for help in finding out where I actually was and how to get back.

"Uh, excuse me, sir. I think I might be lost. Could you please help me find my way back to Holly Street?"

The man looked up from his newspaper with narrowed eyes, a sly smile spreading across his greasy face. His gaze lingered on my body for just a moment too long, making me feel uncomfortable and realizing I had made yet another mistake by coming in when I didn't know the store at all. He leaned a little, his gaze bright and creepy.

"Well, well, what do we have here, huh? Are you a lost little girl all alone in the city?" He asked me, his voice dripping with creepy intent and sarcasm. "This ain't the right part of town for you, girl."

My heart was racing in my chest, and a surge of anger replaced the fear that felt heavy inside of my body. I put my shoulders back and raised my chin, making sure not to let the gross man in front of me intimidate me. I was a grown woman and I was capable.

"I really don't have time for your games, okay? I just need directions to get back to my fiancé's house," I told him, my voice steady but tight with annoyance. The annoyance was easier to feel than the fear that was starting to choke me. The fiancé thing was something I thought might protect me if he knew I had a man waiting for me.

The convenience store worker chuckled at my words, his gaze turning even more sinister as he stared at me. It was obvious he didn't take me very seriously.

"How about you come back here with me? I'll take you home," he said, and I felt sick. "We can be good friends."

"I'll just be on my way," I said, tripping backward as he came around the counter. "I don't need your help anymore—"

He reached out as quickly as a striking snake and he grabbed my lower arm, his grip tightening until it hurt. My heart was pounding in my chest, and I struggled to break free from his grip on me. I couldn't believe that I had managed to get myself into such a terrifying situation. Yeah, it wasn't my fault that I was in trouble, but still.

Just as I was about to shout for help, to scream my fear out into the world even if no one could hear it, a familiar voice cut through the bright tension. I felt relief burn me up.

"Let her go! Take your hands off of her right now!"

I turned my head quickly enough to make my neck crack and I saw Scott, standing with his feet half in and half out at the entrance of the convenience store. His handsome face was filled with a mix of concern and anger that I had never seen before. He seemed to be vibrating with energy, ready to blow. He looked back and forth between me and the man, and then his grip on me. He rushed at us in the store, his presence furious.

"Scott, help—" I began, my voice choked with fear.

"Daisy," was all he said, letting my name fall from his lips like an invocation.

He took four long strides across the store and forcefully pushed the man away from me with a hard push of his hands. His eyes were nearly blazing with fury, the blue as bright as the edge of hot flame. I had never imagined that Scott could look so full of that kind of emotion, and I felt surprised. The man holding me stumbled backward at the shove that Scott gave him, taken aback by Scott's sudden arrival and his apparent determination to get me away from the man that was harassing me in the store.

"You need to step back away from her and get lost before I call the police," Scott warned the man, pointing at him with his voice sharp and filled with authority that neither of us could ignore. "Actually, that's a good idea. I'm sure your store will benefit from the attention the cops will give it."

"Call them," he said, but his voice was shaking. "Call the cops and tell them how she came in here and harassed me in my place of business."

"You're such a liar," I said, my voice trembling with the way my body was shaking.

Scott was pressed against my side, a protective, comforting presence. I found my strength with him there and I felt myself begin to feel safe again. I knew for sure that he wouldn't let anyone hurt me while he was there.

"I would imagine a man like you has some priors," Scott said, his voice low and dangerous. "Let's see who they believe."

To my surprise, Scott actually did call the cops. He put an arm around me, putting himself between me and the store owner. The man, realizing he was outnumbered and his options were limited, quickly retreated from us, slinking behind the counter to gather up his own phone. I wondered who he might be calling but I couldn't really bring myself to care at the moment. I let out a breath I hadn't even realized had been stuck in my throat, feeling a rush of relief as it began to wash over my whole body.

Scott twisted towards me, his expression going soft as he turned and reached out to touch my cheek gently. His touch fell away after a moment that was way too short, and I missed it right away. He was looking at me, looking as if he was wondering if I would break. I wasn't going to though. I could deal.

"Are you okay? You look so pale," Scott said, staring at me with concern etched on his face. "Daisy, I'm so sorry for how everything happened earlier. I shouldn't have let you walk out that door," he told me, his voice filled with genuine relief and remorse.

I felt the tears begin to well up in my eyes as the adrenaline started to fade even more than it already did, leaving me feeling way too vulnerable and almost entirely emotionally drained because of it. I felt like I could sleep for ages. I nodded at him, unable to find the words to help him understand the rough mix of emotions swirling inside me like a hurricane over the ocean.

"It's okay," Scott told me, and imagined he didn't speak so gently very often. "You're okay."

Scott pulled me into a comforting embrace, holding me tightly as if to shield me from any more harm. At that moment, I realized that despite whatever our differences may have been and our arguments, he really seemed to care about me. The thought of it made my heart thump quickly in my chest.

"Cameron?" I asked, looking behind him as if the little boy would be standing there.

"The housekeeper forgot her keys and I paid her extra to stay with him while I went to find you," he told me. "You shouldn't have run out like that," he said as he pulled away from me.

"I didn't just run out," I told him, looking up and feeling defensive. The guy behind the counter was still huddled back there, and I realized he must have tried to get out through the other door, but we were blocking both exits where we were standing. I nodded, "That guy is trying to get out."

"I don't care about that guy," Scott said dismissively. He called loudly, "The cops will be here to pick him up in about four minutes. I want to know why you thought it was okay."

I heard the creepy man groan, sinking into a chair behind the counter, accepting fate.

"Like I said, I didn't just run out, but you didn't care to try and understand what I was saying," I told him, crossing my arms. I felt the familiar cold, detached attitude come over Scott again. It made me feel sick. "Your son matters more than any job, I'll tell you that. He's going to remember the time you spent with him and the time you didn't."

"Yeah well, you didn't set a very good example for Cameron running out like that, and that's what you were hired for," he said, shoving his hands into his pockets. How quickly we had spiraled.

"Yeah, that's all I'm sticking around for," I snapped, turning on my heel and heading to his car.

In the distance, police sirens screamed through the streets. Blue lights silhouetted the figure of Scott Wilson, tall and forlorn in the darkened doorway.

Penny was going to have a meltdown.

Chapter 9

Scott

I stood in the kitchen, the aroma of freshly brewed coffee lingering in the air. The tension was palpable as I watched Daisy move around the room, her movements brisk and purposeful. She wasn't looking at me and she hadn't looked up one time since I found her in the kitchen, looking over Cameron's assignments, early this morning. The silence between us was deafening, broken only by the clinking of coffee cups and the sound of the brewing machine. I thought about it and I cleared my throat, trying to find the right words to break through the wall of resentment that had built up between us.

"Daisy, can we talk?" I asked her, my voice colored with the growing burn of frustration and worry that we would never be the same again. Something about Daisy brought out emotion in me that I had tamped down on for years. "At least tell me if you're okay after last night. I know you were pretty shaken up."

Daisy paused just for a moment and then she continued what she was doing, her back turned to me on purpose so that she didn't have to make eye contact with me. She didn't respond to, and her purposeful silence spoke volumes about how she felt about the situation. It was pretty clear that she was still annoyed with me, and her refusal to talk to me about anything only fueled my need to resolve the issue between us.

"I understand that you're upset with me," I told her as I continued, keeping my voice steady and calm. "But you have to understand that expanding the oil company is necessary for the growth and future success of my business. It's not an easy decision to make, but it's one that needs to be made and I'm the one to do it."

Daisy finally turned to face me, her eyes filled with a mixture of disappointment and anger. I hated the feeling that look gave me, making me heavy with displeasure. She had a way about her like no one else ever had. Instead of pushing me to move forward, she was pulling me back and wanting me to stand still. It was the strangest thing.

"Scott, you have to listen to me. You are so focused on your work that you're all but neglecting your son when he needs you," she told me, her voice laced with sadness. "Cameron needs you right now, and I think he deserves more of your time and attention. I know I haven't been here very long, but even I can see that."

The way her words hit me like a punch to the gut was actually shocking. I knew what she thought of me already, but to tell me I was neglecting my boy was distressing. Daisy wasn't the kind of person to lie and try to trick anyone. I was the one that had her lying for my benefit in the first place. I loved my son so much, and the thought of him feeling like I was letting him down tore at the strings of my heart. I knew she was partly right, but I also knew that the expansion of the company was seriously needed for our financial stability and the opportunities that would add up for Cameron in the future.

"I'm doing all of this for him, Daisy," I replied, my voice filled with a mixture of defensiveness and desperation. "I want to give him the best possible life, with all the opportunities that come with it. But in order to do that, I have to work hard and make sacrifices."

Daisy's face seemed to soften for a moment, her rich brown eyes searching mine.

"I know and I understand that, Scott," she told me, her voice soft and gentle now. "But there has to be a balance between all of that and you need to figure out what's most important to you. Cameron needs his father, not just material things that he won't even care about once it's all said and done. He needs quality time with you and your presence rooted deeply in his life would solve a lot of his problems, I think."

The things she said did make a lot of sense to me. I knew she was genuine in what she felt and how much she wanted both of us to be there for Cameron. In her eyes, I had been so preoccupied with my work and my goals that I had lost sight of what genuinely mattered to me. My son needed me not only as someone to look after him and put food on the table but also as a caring and mindful father.

"Look, I hear you, Daisy," I told her, my voice filled with cautiousness. "And I promise you, I will try and make changes where it really matters. I'm not who you think I am and I'm going to find a way to balance my job and be there for my son."

Daisy looked at me, and her eyes were searching for sincerity. After a moment, she nodded, a thin smile stretching at the corners of her lips. "I genuinely hope you mean what you say, Scott," she told me quietly. "Cameron deserves nothing less than your best effort. Change for him. Be better."

With those last words hanging heavy in the air, Daisy turned and made her way out of the kitchen, leaving me there alone, the weight of my life heavy on my head. I took a deep breath, trying very hard to gather my thoughts and find a way to reassess this.

"You're a grown man," I muttered to myself. "Figure it out."

I couldn't help but feel determined as I made my way to my home office. Perhaps I did need to genuinely reconsider the choices I was making. I had never felt so conflicted in my life. I went up to my computer, opened my calendar, and began reorganizing my next few days. I outsourced some of my responsibilities, postponed a few of my appointments, and promised myself that I would prioritize my son's well-being over everything else. I knew it wouldn't be easy, and there would be challenges along the way, but I was willing to make the necessary choices to be the father that Cameron really needed. I hoped I would be able to sacrifice for him when it came down to it. Daisy made a good point.

A sense of anticipation and resolve poured over me as I glanced at the new calendar I had shifted around. I knew there was a long road ahead of me, but I was going to try and force myself to take the first step. I closed my eyes and imagined Cameron and I in the future, creating a bond that would last a lifetime. I regretted not having a bond with my own father and I didn't want to make the same mistakes with my son.

As I sat in my office, the morning sunshine streamed through the window, creating a warm and inviting glow on the mahogany desk in front of me, I felt better about everything. The familiar aroma of freshly made coffee coupled with the perfume of leather from the recliner I was sitting in was very comforting. It was going to be another hectic day at the office, as my oil company's growth was supposed to start in another location very soon. But before I could even consider it and decide what I was going to do about it in the long run, I needed to gather my thoughts and mentally prepare myself for the day ahead.

I was sipping my coffee, immersed in my thoughts, when I heard hasty footsteps approaching the open door of my office. I looked up to see my son Cameron, his school bag slung over his shoulder, standing in the doorway with a wide grin on his face.

"Dad, guess what? You'll never guess, it's so cool!" He exclaimed in his high voice, barely able to contain his excitement at whatever he was about to say.

I gave him a smile, putting my coffee mug down. "What's going on, Cam?" I asked my son, already thinking that I knew his answer.

He only got this excited about school projects and functions. He loved school, just not the rules that went along with it. Cameron was a bright and imaginative young boy, and he had always been enchanted by the fun of being in his elementary school. While his classmates probably easily followed the strict routines, Cameron's mind wandered to the endless possibilities beyond the walls of the school. He was like me in that way. I hoped he wasn't like me in all ways though. I had never quite found a way to balance my father's softness and my grandfather's drive that battled for power in my mind daily. The world was my son's canvas, willing and waiting to be painted with the bright colors of whatever his dreams turned out to be.

"There's going to be a scavenger hunt at school in a few days!" Cameron told me, bouncing excitedly on the balls of his feet. "All of the other kids on the group chat online are talking about it, and I can't wait to go! Can you see if Ms. Mullins thinks it's okay?"

"I'm sure it's fine," I told him honestly. "She wants you to participate. Are you finishing all of your work and getting everything done?"

"Daisy is helping me," he nodded, grinning. "So we can go then?"

I winced to myself and couldn't help but feel a cold pang of guilt. Hadn't I just told Daisy that I would make changes and include myself in Cameron's life more? Was I really going to go back on my word so quickly? With my busy schedule and constant focus on work, I sometimes missed out on the smaller moments with my son, but I always tried to make it up to him.

"Yeah, that seems like a lot of fun, Cam," I told my son, trying to hide the fact that I was conflicted in the tone of my voice. "I'm sure you're going to have a great time."

Cameron's smile went wide and his familiar blue eyes gleamed with excitement.

"It's actually a father-son scavenger hunt," he said, looking a little more shy than he usually did. "I think we're supposed to do it together. Do you think you can?"

"I have to get on a call, bud, can you go wait in the living room for me to finish up?" I asked him, though I didn't need to make a phone call. I just needed time to think.

I looked up at the calendar on my computer, glancing over it. My heart sank as I quickly learned the scavenger hunt overlapped with the company's planned growth. It was a critical time for the business as a whole, and my presence was essential. I told Daisy I would try, but obviously, as soon as the heat was on me, I was ready to fold and keep my commitments to my job. As I considered both the benefits and negative outcomes, the decision weighed relentlessly on my mind. On the one hand, having a presence in my son's life was something I cherished and valued. I wanted to be involved with his life, to support him, and to make memories with him when I could. The scavenger hunt presented us with an opportunity to bond, and I couldn't deny how important that was to me. On the other side, the expansion of the company was a high bar I needed to meet.

I walked out of my home office and I found Cameron waiting happily in the hallway. I nodded at him, putting a hand on his shoulder. He looked so much like me.

"I've made my decision, Cam," I told him.

Chapter 10

Daisy

I had been avoiding Scott for three days.

I drew in a long breath as I went into the bustling store, the bright lights illuminating the aisles filled with familiar school supplies. We were going to get a nice lunch afterward and it was going to be a good day. I talked to Penny the night before, and she made me feel better. I didn't want to worry about Scott. He was a grown man. I forced myself to stop thinking about how I needed to change his mind. I was going to let the chips fall where they may, but it was really difficult. That was why I was just ignoring Scott. I focused on shopping. The air was filled with the scent of freshly situated supplies and the excitement of the children preparing for the upcoming scavenger hunt at the school. Today I was helping and taking Cameron to get a few supplies for the event.

"Are you ready?" I asked Cameron. "Do you have the list for the stuff that you need?"

Cameron's eyes darted around the store, wandering ahead of me in his bright sneakers, cartoon t-shirt, and shorts. I watched him carefully. Cameron's usually cheerful and sunny attitude seemed clouded with a dark cloud of sadness, and I couldn't help but feel a pang of worry for him. I did care about him and it wasn't about keeping my job safe. Cameron was a complicated kid and he even told me about his mom leaving him with his dad a year or so earlier. It explained a lot of his behavior in my eyes and it was what made me push even harder for Scott to step in and fill both parental roles for his son.

"Hey, are you alright up there?" I asked him lightly, catching up to him. "What's wrong?"

He kicked the tiles with the toe of his sneaker. I had never seen him look so down.

He let out a sigh, his voice barely rising above a whisper. "I don't think I need these supplies anymore," he told me, his bright eyes going dim. "It would just be a waste."

I was surprised by his sudden change of heart and I stopped right there in my tracks, making a few shoppers around the same aisle to give us curious looks. He had been so excited a few hours ago and though he had talked to his dad again, it hadn't seemed like he was upset afterward. I wondered what it was that made him sad all of a sudden.

"What do you mean, Cam?" I asked him, and even I could hear that my voice was heavy with genuine worry for him. "Did something happen? Is that kid from school bothering you somehow?"

"No, we're friends now. I told you we made up," he told me, shaking his head.

"Well, what is it then? You can trust me," I said, coming to look at him. "If something is going on, maybe I can help."

He waited for a minute before finally talking again. His voice was very, very sad.

"I shouldn't have looked, but I saw my dad's computer calendar. I know he won't be able to come to the father-son scavenger hunt tomorrow," he admitted to me in a voice that was wracked with emotion. "Maybe I shouldn't have asked him. I knew he couldn't."

My heart felt heavy as I listened intently to Cameron's words. I knew just how much he had been looking forward to the occasion, and he had been eager to spend some quality time with his father. Scott should have realized that but he always seemed to miss the important things. He wasn't what he should have been when it really mattered. The fact that his father would be unable to be there was definitely crushing to his little heart. Anger surged through my body, targeted at Scott once again. The man was infuriating. How could he have let his son down so badly once again? I didn't think it was even the first time he had gone back on a promise to Cameron, but this one seemed especially hard to me. I took in a long breath and tried to gather my thoughts before speaking to Cameron again.

"Oh, I'm so sorry to hear that," I told him, making sure my voice was even with empathy. "But you know what, Cam? You don't even need a scavenger hunt to have fun, though I think you'll still go. We can have our own adventure right at home, you'll see."

Cameron looked up at me. He seemed conflicted between hope and sadness. It tugged at my heart to see him looking that way. He was such a sweet kid most of the time.

"Really? Do you think so?" He asked me. "My dad said he made up his mind but he wouldn't tell me what he meant. I know that means it's a no."

Of course Scott told him something like that. He probably approached the conversation with his son like it was a business meeting.

"Yeah, of course," I told him. "Me and my dad used to make macaroni necklaces and pine cone table dressings. Does that sound fun?"

Cameron nodded. "I've never done that. Do other kids do that?"

"I would think so," I told him, and I felt another pang of sadness for him. "Maybe after, you can teach other kids who don't know how."

Cameron grinned. "I can do that!"

We grabbed the rest of the supplies for the scavenger hunt and then we filled the buggy with bags of macaroni noodles and yarn. There were stacks of pinecones wrapped netting in the craft section and we put a few in the cart as well. Cameron picked sunflowers from the shelf to glue to the pinecone table pieces, grinning at me as I shook my head, smiling.

"Do you think we can ask Dad to help?" Cameron asked from the back of the car. We were back inside of the black Tahoe that Scott told me to use whenever I wanted.

"Sure we can ask," I said, but my tone was bitter. "I won't make any promises though."

I saw Cameron nod in the rearview mirror, looking sad again. I turned back to look at the road and squeezed my hands on the steering wheel. Scott and I were going to have a little heart-to-heart.

"Can I carry the bags into the house?" Cameron asked me, nearly bouncing on the balls of his feet once we were back home. I was glad to see him happy, if only for a moment.

"Sure can," I told him, reaching out and ruffling his hair. "Take these into the kitchen and then go finish your homework. I'll make you some lunch. Peanut butter and strawberry jelly?"

"Yes, please!" He called over his shoulder at me as he hurried into the house with his arms full of bags.

I smiled, shaking my head. I looked at the house, tall and imposing in front of me. Even though it was sunny outside, I could see that it looked like the light was on in Scott's office. I steeled myself and stomped my way into the house. Cameron was nowhere to be found and I had a bone to pick with the man of the house.

"What do you think you're doing?" I said, sailing into the open doorway of his office with my hair flying.

"Daisy," he said, looking up in surprise. "What are you talking about? Come in here and sit down," he muttered, gesturing to the chair in front of his desk.

"No, I don't want to sit down," I snapped, rubbing a hand over my eye where a headache was beginning to throb under the skin. "You did it again, Scott."

"What did I do?" He asked, raising his eyebrows.

"You know Cameron was really looking forward to this scavenger hunt. Don't worry though, we're making macaroni jewelry now," I said flatly.

"Macaroni?" He asked me, his face pinched in confusion. "What does macaroni have to do with anything?"

"It doesn't matter!" I snapped once again. "None of it matters because you won't show him the attention he needs. You're stuck."

"I'm not stuck," he told me easily.

He leaned back in his chair, stretched his muscled arms above his head and strained his dress shirt. I could feel myself unable to stop watching him as he did so. He stood up and walked over to stand in front of me, looking tall and insanely attractive. I pushed it aside and tried not to think about him or smell that amazing cologne that he used. It took a lot of self-control on my part.

"You're crazy is what you are," I told him easily. I threw my hands up. "Your son gives you chance after chance to make things right and you throw it back in his face nearly every time. He's making an effort and you should too. It's not fair to him in the slightest."

I just felt so bad for poor Cameron, who just wanted to live up to his father's big life. He wanted spend time with his father, but Scott was someone who would only ever care about how much money he made, even when he didn't need it for anything.

"I know how hard he's trying," Scott said, nodding. "I know who he is and I'm proud of him."

"How can you be proud of him when you haven't seen him? How could you tell him you were going to go, making him so excited about the scavenger hunt and then you go and schedule something with that new expansion on the day you're supposed to do the hunt with Cameron." My voice sounded tight, but I was well aware. "And on that line of thought, another thing I want to talk about is—"

Scott's warm, pliant mouth cut me off as he planted a firm kiss on my lips. His hands cradled my face and when he leaned his forehead against mine, I felt an overwhelming feeling of *right*. We were finally blossoming into something more and I liked it, but I still felt the same anger that I did before. I pulled back away from him and he sighed, but he was smiling.

"I canceled the expansion, if you must know," he said, looking unsure and yet very proud of himself. "It's halted until next year. Despite what you may think, I do put my son first over everything. Thank you for making me see what was right."

"So, the scavenger hunt?" I asked him, watching him carefully and thinking of being kissed by him again. "Are you actually going to go or are you just saying that?"

"My schedule is all cleared up," he told me, his hands on my waist. He grinned down at me. "I'm even free for some macaroni."

"Are you serious?" I asked him. I felt a warmth blossoming in my chest. Cameron was going to be so excited.

He nodded, pointing. "Go look in that office closet over there. You'll have your answer."

I went over warily, opening the wooden door of the closet. Inside, I realized that he had all the same supplies that we had. He was going to do the scavenger hunt with Cam.

"I'm proud of you," I told him. "You're going to make his life so much easier. You know he was acting out to try and get your attention. He just needed someone to listen."

"You're good for him," Scott told me. "What do you think about doing full-time?"

"As a nanny?" I asked him, surprised.

He nodded. "I know you want the cover model thing, but you'll make the right choice."

"I don't need to," I told him with a shrug. "I wanted to be a model for my mom, but I'm realizing that I don't have to be unhappy to make her proud. She was already proud."

Scott nodded, giving me a warm look. He came back to me, pulling me in close.

"I was thinking," he began, kissing me again, "maybe you could make this a permanent thing. Maybe you don't have to find a new place."

"What are you saying?" I asked him, my heart soaring with affection.

"What I'm saying, Daisy Gray, is will you marry me?" Scott asked me, wrapping his arms around me. "What do you say, sunflower? Are you ready to do this thing, for real this time?"

I said yes, with great excitement. This was where I was meant to be, in his arms as his wife forever.

THE END

If you like this book
you'll LOVE my next book, "Billionaire's New Love."
Here is a little blurb for you.

I avoided a bad mistake by running from my cheating Ex during our wedding.

Now I'm working for a grumpy, billionaire, single dad, who may be my worst mistake *ever*.

I was hired to be a nanny and now I am a billionaire's fake wife!

One burnt meal and I thought I was going to be fired. Instead, I saw a twinkle in his eyes I didn't think he was capable of expressing.

I just needed a job and now my heart palpitated with excitement every time he looked at me.

I tried to keep Scott at arm's length, but I've hit the wall of reality. He is much older than me and he's my boss!

I need to focus on grooming him to be a better father to a wild child only until he gets me a connection to a modeling agency as he promised.

Printed in Great Britain
by Amazon